Soul Mates

~for eternity~

By D.S. Baze

Lulu.com Publishing
March 2011

Table of Contents

Preface

Hello! I'm D.S.Baze. I am a wife, a mother, and a chronic daydreamer. I started writing in high school. I usually wrote dumb little things to catch people's attention or to entertain. In 1993 it took a more serious turn. I was in counseling and turned to writing as a way to heal. I found I could express my own emotions and thoughts more thoroughly through my characters. That is how my book "Soul Mates" was born. My first writing of it was a milder version. I wanted younger kids to be able to read it. In 2009 an old high school friend, who is a published author, came back into my life and strongly encouraged me to pick it back up and edit it. In that process I ended up re-writing many parts for the more mature readers and changed the ending. When I finished, I realized my true vision, to give hope to young women trying to find a way to heal themselves.

Acknowledgements

I thank God every day for my husband and daughters. They have truly made my life complete. My husband has been by my side since I was a teenager. He has encouraged me to be the best person I can be from day one. He taught me how to trust and how to love. He will always be the love of my life. I was blessed with two amazing daughters who allowed me to better understand God's unconditional love. From the time they were born it changed my view on life. All I ever wanted was to be the best mom I could for them. They gave me a purpose in life when I felt I really didn't have one. Kurt, Brandy, and Kirsty, all three of you are my world.

Since this book took seventeen years from start to finish, there are so many people who helped me along the way. I don't have room to list everyone so I will focus on a few key players. I thank my counselor, Mary Haley. With her guidance I was able stop the nightmares that haunted from the time I was 16 until I was 28 years old. With her I was able to reach a new level of maturity and emotional healthiness.

To all my students I am thankful. I am especially thankful for the kids who were sixth graders at Perkins-Tryon Middle School in 1993. I taught a Humanities Class in which I read aloud the beginnings of this book. They gave me input on what would keep their attention. They gave me the encouragement I needed to keep writing. (The first writing of this did not include the explicit language and was not as detailed.) They had no idea how much they were helping me heal.

Another person who was vital to this book getting out to the world was C. Tyler Storm. She and I attended junior high and high school together. We went separate ways for many years then our lives crossed paths again in 2009. She had just published her own novel and offered to help me pursue my dream of being an author. I had left this book alone all those years. With her encouragement I pulled it back out and started editing it. In the process, I realized I had grown emotionally. I had also raised two daughters and knew I had to make more of an effort in my writing to help my main character. I truly believe it was all part of God's perfect timing.

The last person I will thank by name is JoAnna Rasp. She gave me powerful insight which encouraged me to take the final step and submit this manuscript. She was the last piece of this puzzle and entered my life at just the right time.

Again, there are so many people who helped me along the way that it humbles me. Even if I didn't write your name in this space, it doesn't mean I have forgotten. If you encouraged me, accepted me, or loved me, I thank you. I thank you for being a part of my life!

Chapter 1

The Broken Promise

Jessica struggled as she clung to her belongings with one hand. She had an oversized purse, several textbooks, a couple of binders, some notepads, and her car keys. She carefully tapped in the code to disarm the security system with her free hand. Even though she had taken tests in two classes that day and didn't have any homework in them, her other teachers seemed to pick up the slack. The schedule she chose for her sophomore year of high school was going to push her to her limits; that was for sure.

Pressing the last button on the control panel made the light on it switch from red to green. With the alarm off she was able to use both of her hands to carry everything into the house. She clumsily made it through the front door and dropped her keys in the bowl that sat on a table in the hall. She immediately went to her bedroom and closed her door. She had never really gotten used to living in such a large house. She was an only child so she really didn't see the need for her family to have five bedrooms, but it was very important to her father to have the finest of everything. He liked to show off their wealth. At times Jessica did too, but coming home to a gigantic house all alone was not on her list of favorite things to do, especially since she couldn't lock her own bedroom door.

It was a Tuesday and both her parents were gone. Her mother would be gone the rest of the day since she had a group of friends that met every week. Together they would take a road trip in order to find something new or exciting. Their trips were to shopping malls in different cities, symphonies, museums, plays, or sometimes they would just go visit people, like an old high school buddy or someone else from their past. Whatever they wanted to do, they did. The three women had been friends since they were in elementary school, and they remained close their entire adult lives. Jessica always thought it was a great idea to travel with friends like that, and thought she might do the same someday herself with a group of her own friends. She just didn't know what friends that would be. She wasn't like her mother in that respect. Jessica thought of herself as kind of a loner. She was popular at school, but she never really had a best friend for more than a year. She was always focused on school and sports. In her spare time she loved being alone to listen to music or write poetry. People would invite her to do things, but for some reason she was just never motivated to go out.

Jessica looked at the time. It was 3:45 P.M. She needed to remember to start supper preparation for her father around 5:30 pm so it would be ready by 6:30 pm. She never knew exactly when he would be home, but he was always ready to eat at *exactly* 6:30 pm. She started to set her alarm but decided she didn't need it; surely she would remember. She did this every Tuesday. She would just follow whatever directions for supper her mother had laid out. The meals were always simple. It was never a problem.

The afternoon sun lit up her room and the warmth embraced Jessica like a blanket. She loved a warm room. Sorting through her homework she decided to read the assigned chapter from the novel given to her for her English Class. She was certain there would be a quiz tomorrow to find out who read it and who didn't. She always did all of her homework. She was a straight "A" student and wouldn't settle for anything less. After she finished the chapter, she would move on to either her math or anatomy homework. She loved her English class, was fine with her math class, but dreaded her anatomy class. That was her hardest class this semester.

Jessica stacked up several pillows on her bed. She fluffed them all, then took her book and sat right in the middle of them. She started to read. She had heard from the upper classmen who had read it that it was a good book, but she was starting the first chapter and it seemed to drag on. Of course, all new books seem to start out slowly before you learn the characters' names and what the story is about. This book, though, was especially hard because nothing grabbed her interest to begin with. There was just so much detail.

Sleep deprivation from last night's study session, a long day at school, the warm temperature of the room, combined with a reading a book she wasn't captured by yet were not a good combination. With every word Jessica's eyelids became heavier and heavier. Sleep was trying to overtake her.

She realized she was getting really sleepy so she hopped up and grabbed a brush. "One hundred strokes," she said to herself. That's what someone had told her, if she brushed her hair one hundred times each day it would grow faster. Jessica sleepily gazed at her reflection in the mirror as she ran the brush through her hair. Her long blonde hair was straight and had grown quite a bit since she had been brushing it so much. It hung down several inches past her bra strap, and when she pulled it forward it touched the bottom of her rib cage. It seemed everyone else had curly or permed hair and fixed it crazy ways. Most girls had bangs they would make stand up as well. Popular 80's hairstyles just didn't seem to match her taste. Jessica felt a little out of the loop in that area, but she was just fine with her straight hair. It was probably the feature she liked most about herself. It set her apart from others.

After brushing her hair one hundred times she returned to her bed to read once more. She glanced over at the clock and it was only 4:15 pm. Several minutes into it she felt her eyelids getting heavy again. She tried to push through. The book was a bit difficult to read, and she couldn't fight off how tired she was. Within minutes she lost the battle and was fast asleep.

The silence was broken by the roar of her father's voice, "Jessica! Jessica! Jessica Ann Taylor, get your ass in here right now!"

"I'm coming, Dad."

Jessica's heart raced as her body filled with adrenaline. She looked at the clock and realized she had overslept. She failed to make supper on time. She jumped to her feet and quickly walked to the living room. As she entered the doorway, she watched the smoke from her father's pipe linger in the air forming a cloud near the ceiling. He was facing the opposite wall. The cloud would swirl a moment then gradually disappear until new smoke joined in. She tried to avoid her father as much as possible on these Tuesday nights when her mother was gone. Her father's temper always seemed shorter, and his drinking much worse. Tonight was no exception.

Jessica stood trembling in silence and studied his body language. His tie was loosened around the collar of his snow white starched shirt, and his sleeves were haphazardly folded up. His hair, which had once been neatly combed, was now standing in different directions as though he had run his hands through it several times. He tapped an impatient finger against his leather chair.

There was a half empty glass bottle sitting next to him on the end table, a bottle that had been full of some sort of alcohol earlier. Beside that was a glass filled with a few ice cubes and a touch of the alcohol that was in the bottle. She was afraid to break the silence and let him know she had entered the room and was standing behind him, yet she knew she had to before he yelled again.

"What do you need, Dad?" she asked, her voice somewhat hoarse. Mr. Taylor abruptly turned his head so his eyes could glare at hers. The sudden movement made Jessica's heart jump yet again.

"Where is my gawddamn supper?" he demanded.

"Supper?!" Jessica replied. "I'm so sorry. I fell asleep doing my homework." Jessica glanced at the clock on the nearest wall. It read 6:31 p.m. She couldn't believe she had fallen asleep and didn't make supper. She was angry at herself for not setting an alarm.

Mr. Taylor's eyes grew dark as he tightened his jaw. "You what? You know damned well we eat at precisely 6:30 every night. Every night I expect my food to be on that fucking table. Not before, not after, but at 6:30. THAT'S THE RULE! It's my job to bring home the money and your or your mother's job to make sure the house is clean and my supper is served. How could you be so stupid and forget about something we do every gawddamn night? Well? Answer me!" He replied through clenched teeth.

"I'm really sorry," Jessica explained as she tried to swallow the lump that was forming in her throat. It wouldn't go away. She didn't mean to fall asleep. She really didn't. Her father never listened when he was angry, so she didn't want to tell him she had a ton of homework tonight and had spent all last night studying, too. Tomorrow she had that chapter due plus a serious anatomy test. She hadn't even had a chance to study for that yet. Her anatomy teacher, Mrs. Finnegan, was one of those high school teachers who really should have been a college professor. She made things more difficult than they really needed to be. But that was beside the point right now. Right now she had to face the consequences of falling asleep and not having supper on the table.

"How could you fall asleep in the middle of the afternoon? You don't even work! All you do is go to school. School is *nothing* compared to the life in the real world. You are just a lazy little whore that doesn't do what she's told!" Mr. Taylor yelled at her, his temper finally exploding. He took hold of the half empty bottle and slammed it into the lifeless fireplace. The bottle shattered on impact making Jessica tremble.

He rose out of his chair and stood within an arm's length of Jessica. His breath smelled heavily of alcohol as he continued his rant, "You know the rule in this house. Children who do *not* do what they are told are to be *punished*! You were instructed to have supper on the table at exactly 6:30, and you fell asleep for some god forsaken reason. You disobeyed! No child that bares my last name will be allowed to be disobedient. I won't let you grow up to be like your mother's side of the family. I refuse to let that happen. I am too important in this damn community and people know me here. If you are a failure, it only looks bad on me. I have worked too fucking hard to let that happen! No one, not even you, will tarnish my good name and what I have built here. I did it by working my ass off and having an impeccable work ethic. I don't just sit around listening to music or talking on the phone and ignoring what needs to be done like you. Now remove your pants! By god I will teach you with my belt how to be responsible!"

"No, Dad! I didn't mean to disobey. Honest. You don't understand! I have so much homework, and I stayed up all night last night studying!" Jessica reacted by screaming back, watching as Mr. Taylor angrily removed the belt from his trouser and folded it once in half, gripping the buckle with the loose end. He lunged forward grabbing her by the forearm. His hand squeezed Jessica so tightly that tears formed in her eyes as all her muscles constricted. "Don't you ever talk back to me like that!" he hissed. "Do what you are told. *Now!*" This demand came as he jerked her arm then shoved her away from him.

Jessica stumbled back, barely keeping her balance. When she was younger she had tried running away from him a few times. Soon she learned that was not the answer. Running from him only made the punishment worse. She would get hit for disobeying, and then she would get hit for running. The only thing she felt she could do when it got to this point was to obey his instructions and to hope that it would be over quickly. He was bigger, stronger, and faster. She couldn't fight back no matter how badly she wanted to. She reluctantly slid her pants down to just under her bottom, exposing her underwear. This was not the way her other 16 year old friends were punished. They were grounded from things, not whipped like they were still in elementary school. Deeply humiliated, she clenched her teeth preparing for impact. She hated her father for this. She hated him so much.

Mr. Taylor cast his arm back, narrowed his eyes, and let loose with the belt. Jessica felt the cold leather hit her tender flesh as it made an audible 'smack' that echoed through the room. The initial pain was almost unbearable. Immediately, tears of pain and humiliation welled up in her eyes again. A cry of pain escaped her lips. Her father forcefully grabbed the back of her pants and yanked them until they fell, and pooled around her ankles. Jessica almost lost her balance again. Mr. Taylor's rage-fueled blows violently hit Jessica over and over, landing anywhere from the small of her back to right above the back of her knees. Jessica cupped her hands over her mouth trying to silence her own cries though she couldn't stop the flood of tears. The belt landed again and again. With every blow, Jessica hurt more and more. It got to the point that she thought she couldn't take it anymore or she would pass out. Luckily for her, his tirade came to an end because he physically exhausted himself. When Mr. Taylor had finished, red swollen streaks covered Jessica's body. She tried to control her crying.

Her father walked over to the end table and took his glass of alcohol. He avoided eye contact with her as he left the room mumbling, "You worthless piece of shit. You make me sick. I'll just handle my own supper. If I want anything done right around here I have to do it myself anyway." Jessica didn't know if she was supposed to hear that or not.

Jessica pulled her jeans back up without fastening them, and fled to the safety of her room as tears streamed down her face. Once there, she threw herself on the bed and sobbed some more.

Her mind screamed as she pounded her fists against her mattress, 'I hate you! I hate you! I hate you! I hate you!' Jessica knew that it was horrible to feel that way about her father. Well, actually, he wasn't her biological father, but he was the only father she had ever known. He had married her mother when Jessica was a baby and legally adopted her so they would all three have the same last name. She had no memory of her biological father. He had never tried to make any contact with her. She wondered if he even knew she was alive at all. She wondered if he would hit her the way this father did.

Her mother had barely made it through high school and could not have supported the lifestyle they now had without Mr. Taylor. So Jessica felt thankful for having all the nice things he had provided for the family -- cars, jewelry, plenty of money, vacations to exotic places -- but she hated him at the same time. She hated feeling like she was always at his mercy; however, without him she and her mother would have nothing. He made sure Mrs. Taylor never worked. He made sure she was totally dependent on him and his money. He wanted her to wait on him hand and foot, and she did just that. Jessica swore to herself when she married one day it would be a 50/50 relationship. She vowed not to have a relationship like this one. She would never be someone's servant.

Her tears created little streams that ran down her face to pool at her chin before they fell and landed on Jessica's bed. The physical pain was undeniable, yet the emotional pain ran deeper.

It took about a half hour for the river of tears to run dry. When they came to a stop, Jessica pulled herself up off the bed and walked over to her full-length mirror. Her back stung with every step. She undressed and stood so she could see every mark that was made on her skin. The emotions welled up inside her again, but this time she managed to choke them down. Why couldn't he have been more understanding? Sometimes people make mistakes. She didn't mean to fall asleep. She really didn't. She just was sleep deprived and needed to do her homework. She had to keep good grades in school to stay in the Honor Society and to make it into a prestigious college. Jessica always did her homework right after school. Usually falling asleep wasn't an issue. If she could do it all over again, she would have set an alarm for herself, but she hadn't. Nothing could change that now.

Jessica turned slightly to see the marks more clearly. Long strips of red swollen skin revealed exactly where the belt had landed. As she thought about it, the humiliation returned. She swallowed hard in an effort to push the emotion away. She didn't want to cry any more. She didn't feel she had any tears left anyway. Hatred, anger, and frustration gripped her tightly.

Jessica felt the urge to hit her father the way he had hit her. Life seemed so unfair. Why did she have to stay with him alone on the night he drank the most? Why could adults get away with doing whatever they wanted? Like a caged animal, Jessica felt trapped. She knew there was nothing she could do to change her father. She knew she couldn't run away because the authorities would just bring her right back, and then he would really beat her. He would beat her for running away, and then he would beat her for embarrassing him. The only logical way to get away from him was to leave the day she turned 18. She would move away. It didn't matter where as long as it was as far away as possible – far enough away to shield her from his wrath and control.

Bedtime came early for Jessica. Her only supper consisted of some leftover crackers she had put in her purse from lunch. They had come with a salad she had ordered, but she hadn't eaten them at the time, thank goodness. She drank a paper cup full of tap water from her bathroom faucet to chase away the dry mouth the crackers left behind.

Jessica hurried through some math homework she had brought home, and read over her anatomy notes one time. She knew she needed to study more, but her mind wouldn't allow her to focus. She put her books away and started to get ready for bed. She would just set her alarm, get up extra early, and study in the morning.

After washing her face and brushing her teeth Jessica selected her favorite silk pajamas to sleep in. They felt smooth against her skin as she held them to her cheek. Jessica put them on over her head, and let them slide down over her back; her aching skin appreciated the coolness of the material. Satisfied, she climbed into the comfort of her plush bed, and pulled her oversized down comforter up to her ears. Jessica was emotionally drained and wanted nothing more than to be left alone for the rest of the night. Jessica was drifting in that place between reality and sleep when a noise caused her eyes to fly open and put her brain on high alert. It sounded as though someone was trying to open the door but was having a hard time turning the doorknob. Then the hallway light pierced her room as her door partially creaked open. She snapped her eyes shut. Jessica could sense the light but refused to acknowledge it again. She stayed as still as possible with her eyes closed as she listened. Her heart pounding in her chest threatened to drown out the shuffling of approaching footsteps. Jessica was in no mood to deal with any type of confrontation with her father again. Of course, it could be her mother, but she would figure it out first before she opened her eyes.

"Jessica? Jessica, honey, are you asleep?" Mr. Taylor's voice quivered. It had lost its harshness that it had hours earlier. Jessica did not respond. Mr. Taylor clumsily made his way over to her bed. The air around him was thick with a mingled odor of alcohol and tobacco. It repulsed Jessica, and she cringed as he approached and the foul smell became stronger.

She kept her breathing as shallow as possible, even though the fear was making Jessica's heart race. What did he want now? She didn't think she could take being hit again. Mr. Taylor leaned over and put his hand on Jessica's forehead to move her hair away from her face. She lay frozen. 'Just go away and leave me alone. I hate you! Go away,' she silently screamed in her mind.

Mr. Taylor slowly lowered himself to the bed beside her. He sounded as though he might be crying, but Jessica wasn't for sure. She didn't dare open her eyes to find out.

"I'm sorry, Jessica. Daddy didn't' mean to hurt you. He just wants you to be a good girl. Please forgive me," Mr. Taylor slurred.

Jessica fought the temptation to pretend to wake up and speak to him and accept his apology. Maybe he would just go away. Yet, in the dark corners of her mind (a place she wished did not exist), she knew that probably would not be the case. He had a pattern. First he would beat her, and then as the alcohol wore off, he would feel very remorseful. And then, if Mrs. Taylor weren't around…. Jessica couldn't bring herself to even think about it. She hoped it wasn't going to happen this time. Maybe he would just apologize then leave. Sometimes he would just leave, but most of the times, not.

The next thing she knew he had slid his hand under her blankets.

"Daddy's going to make it up to you," he whispered. "I promise."

His hand found its way to her pajamas. Jessica's mind screamed. She wanted to smack his hand away, but something inside her held her back. Jessica was paralyzed. Her thoughts raced around in her head looking for an escape, but she was the 115 pound prey that had been captured by the 200 pound vicious predator.

Mr. Taylor's drunken hands fumbled around, touching her body in a way a father is not supposed to touch his daughter. He started kissing her neck and she wanted to gag, but she forced herself to think of somewhere else, anywhere else but there. Jessica didn't allow herself to feel anything but numbness. She was aware of his touching her and could tell a difference in his breathing, but she forced her mind to go somewhere else. She couldn't allow herself to be in the moment. She had to disconnect so she pictured herself running to her mother and telling her everything that had happened. Then her mother would hug her and promise to protect her. She saw her mother taking a gun out of her purse and pointing it at her father. Telling him if he ever touched Jessica again she would put an end to it once and for all. He apologized and it was all over. He never touched her again. She saw them both fade into the distance until they were both gone.

Then she saw an ocean of endless waves caressed by a sandy beach. The waves were so powerful. They crashed against rocks that lined some of the beach. Upon impact the ocean would split apart into tiny water droplets that would spray the air. It made the air cool. The air danced and swirled around her head. Her hair joined in the dance. She was walking alone. Yes, all alone with no one around to hurt or humiliate her. It was just the ocean, the beach, the fresh air, and her footsteps. That's all she really wanted - to be alone. She was 18 years old in this fantasy and far, far away. She was happy and free.

The audible sniffle by her father redirected her thoughts. It almost brought her back to the present, but she fought hard to stay detached from her body.

Jessica's thoughts reluctantly returned to a time when she was nine years old. Mr. Taylor had violently beaten her for going to a friend's house without permission. Her friend lived just two doors down. He was drunk and grabbed a switch from a small tree in the front yard. Jerking her off the friend's front porch by her arm, he hit her all the way home with that switch. He hit her anywhere he could reach. She was wearing a dress she had worn to church earlier that morning. He didn't care and seemed to focus his blows on her bare legs.

Then Jessica's mother left to go to the store, and she was left all alone with her father. He entered her room and said he felt so bad about how many marks he had left on her. He apologized.

Jessica struggled to remember what had happened next. Even though she couldn't remember the details, she knew something very bad had happened. Something so bad that he made her promise never to tell anyone about it. He told her that it was her duty as his daughter, and that her mother would be mad at her if she found out. He then went on to make his promise; if she could keep their secret, he would never do it again.

As the obedient daughter she had always been, Jessica never told anyone. She never told anyone because she just knew they would think that she was a bad kid and that somehow she had brought it on herself. Jessica didn't want to be a bad kid. He, on the other hand, had broken his promise multiple times over the years. She always hoped that one day he would keep his promise. It made her angry that he lied. Adults could do whatever they wanted. Adults had all the power. She couldn't wait until she was an adult.

Her father's words shook her back into the present, "Jessica, please forgive me. I ... I'm so sorry. I won't let this happen again, I promise."

Once again his voice sounded sorrowful. Jessica listened as he clumsily got back to his feet and stumbled out of the room. As soon as the door clicked shut, tears flooded Jessica's eyes. She could no longer hold them back as her soul began to cleanse itself of the dirtiness her father thrust upon her once more, that filthy shame of the broken promise.

Chapter 2

Shame

Jessica muffled her cries in her pillow. Her stomach tied itself in a knot reacting to the horrible thing that had just happened. How dare her father violate her like that? She asked herself the same question she always did, 'What should I do now?' she wondered. She thought about telling the school counselor? But, if she did, her ugly secret may be revealed since the counselor had a daughter in the same grade. The daughter might spread it to her friends. All her friends might spread it to their friends. Before long the whole school would know. That was the last thing she wanted!

Should she tell her mother, even though she knew her mother would never stand up to her father? Once when she was younger Mr. Taylor started to hit Jessica and her mother stepped in to stop him. He simply turned on her and beat her, too. After the incident, Mrs. Taylor just cowered down like a mouse to him. That was the only time Jessica ever remembered her mother getting hit. She decided there would be no point in telling her mother about the beatings since some time had passed. Besides, they only happened when her mother wasn't there, and then it wasn't predictable because it wasn't like it was every time she was gone. Mrs. Taylor was small in stature and was a people pleaser. She was even smaller than Jessica who was only 5'2", so there was no way she could ever make Mr. Taylor stop.

Jessica also considered calling the police on

her father. Her father would be furious with her. He, of course, would try to lie his way out of it making her look like a fool. She was sure the police would believe anything he told them. Jessica was afraid of what might happen afterwards if the police just questioned him and let him go. That would be a horrible night indeed.

Even if they did believe her, and they put him in jail, he wouldn't stay there forever. He would eventually get out, and who knows what would happen then. Plus, it might make the news, and then the whole world would know about it. How humiliating would that be? If he went to jail, Mrs. Taylor and Jessica would have no way of supporting themselves. There never seemed to be a "right" answer.

Confused about what to think or do, Jessica threw her blankets back and found her way into her bathroom. Locking the bathroom door behind her, she started running bathwater. The longer she waited for the tub to fill, the more she was aware of how her father's hands scarred her body.

Disgusted, she ripped her pajamas off, threw them on the ground, and jumped into the water before it was fully drawn. She grabbed a bar of soap and started scrubbing. Instinct told her to wash off any traces of his touch. Jessica had jumped in so quickly, that she didn't feel the sting of the water on her back where the belt had left its marks until moments later. She ignored it, and immediately started lathering the soap against her skin. She pressed the bar with its white foam up and down her arms. Nine or ten strokes on the right arm, nine or ten strokes on the left arm, back and forth. With each stroke she pressed harder and harder.

Realizing the bathtub was full, Jessica stopped for a moment and reached up to shut off the water. She then continued to scrub some more. She grabbed a wash cloth that sat on the side of the tub and submerged it in the water. Lifting it up out of the water soaking wet, she used it to wash away the soap. She thought she would feel clean and refreshed. Jessica was repulsed when the feeling of uncleanliness remained.

She dropped the wash cloth in the water and once again took the bar of soap in her hand. She repeated the process scrubbing...and scrubbing...and scrubbing. She focused on her stomach and breasts. Then she moved her legs. With each stroke, she applied more and more pressure. The harder she pressed down, the more release she felt. Tears welled in her eyes again as she tried in vain to wash away his touch, but it had stained her soul. Her skin was starting to turn red and was showing signs of irritation. Subconsciously, Jessica was trying to punish herself for what had happened. Even though she knew it wasn't her fault, she somehow still felt like it was. She allowed it to happen.

After washing several times, she drained the bathtub and turned the shower on as hot as she could stand. She just let the water hit her face and head. She slowly rotated so the water was able to fall down every side of her body, washing clean any soap left behind. After a while the hot water started to run out. Jessica surrendered herself to the fact that it didn't matter how long she stayed in the shower, she would never be clean.

The water turned cold. She reached down and

turned it off. Shivering now, she grabbed a towel off the rack and wrapped it around her exhausted body. She snatched up her silk pajamas from where they were lying in a clump on the floor and then stomped into her bedroom, and jerked open one of her desk drawers. Jessica reached in and pulled out a shiny pair of black handled scissors. Without hesitating she thrust the scissors into the wad of pajamas, blindly shredding them into pieces. They were no longer her favorite clothes to sleep in. They were dirty - filthy dirty - and would never, **ever** be clean again, just like her.

Jessica continued to haphazardly cut and periodically tear the material until nothing was left but a pile of scraps on the floor. She bent down, picked the pile up, and shoved it away in her trash can. Still not completely satisfied, she threw the scissors back into the drawer then marched over to her bed. Jessica gripped the edge of the fitted sheet and tore it off the mattress. She rolled it up into a bundle and set it on the floor next to her feet. She untangled the flat sheet from the comforter and wrapped it around the first sheet. She took both of them and wedged them into the same trash can that held her pajamas. She would deal with them tomorrow, but until then she had to hide them.

Jessica didn't want those sheets ever to touch her again. She took the full trash can to her clothes closet and set it inside. She knew her mother wouldn't look in there. Knowing she had to put sheets back on the bed, Jessica went into her bathroom and forcefully pulled some clean sheets down from the top shelf of the cabinets and remade her bed with a vengeance.

Chapter 3

Aaron

With new sheets and new pajamas, she decided to try and get some sleep. It was 10:30, and she knew her mother wouldn't be home for another hour and a half. Jessica was exhausted. She crawled into bed and pulled the blankets up to her chin once again. Finally, her breathing began to calm down, and Jessica's body surrendered to a restless sleep and her mind escorted her into a dream that allowed her to escape her reality.

The sun's warmth made Jessica smile as she swung back and forth letting the wind rush through her hair. Swinging was her favorite activity at the park. Yet this park was one she had never been to before. It was empty, but Jessica wasn't alone. Birds filled the surrounding trees singing the most beautiful songs. Occasionally one would fly near her, then change its mind about where it wanted to land. The sun was peaking up over the horizon, turning the clouds into an assortment of pale pinks, bright reds, and deep purples that swirled together as the wind playfully pushed the clouds along.

The park was not only unfamiliar to her, but it was built differently than the ones she knew. This park was bordered with the back yards of neatly kept houses, tiny houses much smaller than her own. Even though they were small they were sprinkled with gardens. Some were filled with assorted vegetables in neat rows; others were overflowing with bright fragrant flowers. Jessica thought this park was like a hidden treasure to the neighborhood and it must be kept secret from the rest of the world.

Without warning, a young boy about her age appeared. He walked out from behind a tree into the open. Jessica slowed her swing. The boy continued to approach her. The closer he came, the better she could see him. His hair was a shiny dark brown, very much like the color of dark chocolate. His face was lightly tanned, which made his blue eyes even more beautiful. He was very handsome, yes, very handsome indeed! His striking features and distinct jawline made it impossible for Jessica to divert her eyes from him. His face was familiar but she didn't know who he was. He was tall, maybe about 6 feet, and he had a slender, yet muscular build. As he walked she could tell he was very coordinated and smooth. His confident swagger told her that he must have been some sort of athlete. She noticed his arms in the short sleeve shirt he was wearing. You could tell he must have lifted weights, but not too much. Jessica didn't like the body builder look, but she liked whatever he had.

Her heart skipped a beat as he spoke, "Hello! Do you mind if I swing next to you?"

"No, I don't mind at all," Jessica replied.

She wanted to say more, but the words

just weren't there. All she could do was return his stare. Again, she got the feeling that she knew him, but she was sure she had never met him before.

"My name is Aaron," he began. "I just moved here."

"It's nice to meet you, Aaron, I'm..."

"Jesse, I know who you are," Aaron broke in before she could finish.

The only person who ever called her Jesse was her mother. Her mind started racing. Aaron calmly took a seat in the swing next to Jessica.

"How did you know?" she quickly asked.

"I know a lot about you," Aaron said, flashing the warmest smile she had ever seen.

Jessica wanted to know, "Like what?" she questioned, shooting him a smile of her own.

"Let's see. Your name is Jessica Ann Taylor. You are 16 ½ years old. You are a cheerleader for your local high school. You play tennis and golf on the weekends. You like to write poetry in your spare time. You listen to all kinds of music, anything from pop to classical. You love animals, especially puppies. Your favorite color is midnight blue, and you have a heart of gold." Aaron smiled looking proud of himself.

With her eyebrows raised and her mouth open, Jessica replied, "How do you know all that?"

His smile changed a little as he became

more serious. *"I know everything about you, Jesse."* Aaron lowered his head as his voice softened almost to a whisper, *"I also know your secret. I know about your father. I know how he attacked you tonight -- twice."*

Jessica was stunned. She didn't know what to think. She was surprised, amazed, confused and embarrassed. She lowered her head to stare at the ground. How could she maintain eye contact now? For a moment she was so ashamed. Aaron read her uneasiness.

"I know this sounds strange, but it came to me when I walked up to you. It just flashed in my mind. It was as though our minds were connected for a moment, and you allowed me to see all your memories of who you are and what you love in this world. I saw your past, and I saw your present. I not only saw it, but I could also feel your emotions. I could feel the pain it caused you. I have been waiting for this day for 17 years. I am here to help you through this the best I can. It is my destiny," he explained softly.

As he spoke, Jessica felt something she hadn't felt before. She was relieved that he knew. He rose from the swing and stood in front of her. Extending his right hand, he offered to assist her out of her own swing. When she accepted his offer, he pulled her to a standing position directly in front of him. Their eyes met once again. Jessica again felt something odd, only this time she felt his compassion for her. She felt safe. There was no logic to it, just an overwhelming emotion that flooded her body.

"I am here to help, if you will let me, but not yet. I must go now, but I will see you again -- soon," Aaron reassured her.

He leaned forward, cradled her head in his hands, and ever so gently kissed Jessica's forehead. As he released her, he looked directly into her eyes and smiled. Then he gave her a quick wink as he turned around to leave. He walked to the tree where he had appeared. Jessica was sure in the deepest part of her soul that she knew him. She just didn't know where they would have met. One thing was for sure, when he looked in her eyes all her pain seemed to go away. He made her feel like a new person. He was absolutely amazing. She hoped that they really would see each other again -- soon.

"Aaron..." Jessica called out to him, but he disappeared in the shadows from the tree. He was gone.

Morning came with the buzzing of an obnoxious alarm clock at 4:00 a.m. Jessica forced herself out of bed and walked over to her window. Pulling the curtain aside, she could see the outline of her mother's black Mercedes sitting quietly in the driveway. It was still dark outside, but light from a nearby street lamp allowed some visibility. Jessica dropped the curtain and walked to her bathroom. Halfway there she suddenly remembered her dream, "Aaron," she whispered to herself, "I didn't even get to tell you goodbye." The images of the dream flooded her mind as she continued mechanically to go through her morning routine.

She repeated Aaron's words to herself, "I am here to help, if you will let me." She wondered what exactly he meant by that. How could some guy in her dream help her? The question lingered in her mind along with a million other thoughts about what had happened the night before with her father. She was overwhelmed with it all, but she found the strength to force it from her mind as she began to get out her books in order to finish her homework and studying.

The time flew. Before she knew it, the clock read 6:15. She hurriedly jumped into the shower to wash her hair. Moments later she stepped out, towel dried her hair, and threw it into a pony-tail. She ran to her closet and pulled out a cute pink top, a pair of jeans, and matching hot pink tennis shoes. After throwing them into her cheerleading bag, she rummaged through her dresser for clean bra, underwear, and socks. She threw them into the bag too. Finally, she found her cheerleading practice gear and dressed herself as quickly as she could. Within minutes she was out the door and headed off to school with her bag and books in tow. Neither parent was awake yet, which was fine with her. Because she had cheerleading practice at 7:00, she was leaving earlier than usual.

The cheerleading sponsor had tried to reserve the gym for the girls, but the basketball coach needed it to hold special practices this week with the playoffs coming up. The next largest open space was the hallway in front of the office. It had been widened to allow the students a gathering place between classes. Benches had been built and a few tables had been placed around. It was referred to as the student lounge.

The only problem was that the other students started arriving for school around 8:00 a.m., which meant the last ten to fifteen minutes of cheerleading practice was watched by a crowd of people. Jessica usually didn't mind though. She liked the extra attention and loved performing in front of any crowd, no matter how large or small. All through practice Jessica's mind kept wandering to her mysterious Aaron. Ordinarily, when she dreamed she would wake up and remember only parts of the dream. This dream was different. She could recall every detail and every word. It was so vivid that it almost seemed real.

"Jessica! I said we start on the count of four. You just stood here and didn't' move at all. What is wrong with you this morning? You seem so out of it!" Suzie Madison said in her bossiest voice. Suzie had beaten Jessica out of head cheerleader by only a couple of points. After receiving the title, she acted more like the President of the United States then head cheerleader.

Jessica faked a smile and replied, "Oh, sorry. I didn't get much sleep last night, and I am still not awake. I will get it right this time."

Suzie whirled back around to the starting position and began counting, "One, two, three and four. "

Jessica began on cue even though her mind wasn't completely focused. Practice seemed to drag on and on. Students started arriving and gathered around to watch. Usually that motivated her to jump a little higher or yell a little louder, but not today. She just couldn't shake the memory of her dream. Cheerleading practice came to an end just a few minutes before the bell. The cheerleaders picked up their bags and joined in the rest of the crowd. Jessica hung back picking up her stuff in slow motion. She still ached from the night before, and the practice irritated her skin again. The 8:15 bell sounded signaling everyone to head for class. Suzie, who had left with everyone else initially, fought her way back through the crowd to approach Jessica. Jessica's eyes met hers.

"I'm sorry, Suzie. I don't know what my problem was today. My mind has been in another place."

Suzie's mouth curved up in a smile, "It's okay. We all have 'off' days I was just shocked to see you of all people have one. Are you sure everything is okay?"

Suzie did have her moments when she could be nice. Jessica was glad to see that now was one of them. They had their disagreements at the beginning of the year and didn't talk much, but since Christmas break they were getting along well. The tension that was once there seemed to have subsided almost completely.

"Yes, I'm fine. I'm just really tired. That's all, "Jessica lied.

Suzie turned as if to leave again, and then whirled around to face Jessica.

"Look," she began, "I know it is none of my business, but I have to ask you something. "

The hall was starting to clear showing it was almost time for class to start. Jessica didn't want to be tardy, but she didn't want to be rude to Suzie either. She waited for Suzie to finish.

"Umm. When you were bending over to pick up your bag your shirt came up, and I saw your back. Did you get into a fight or something?" Suzie asked, concern evident in her voice.

Jessica's throat constricted making it hard to breathe for a second. She had to think of something quick. She wouldn't dare tell Suzie the truth. She might spread it all over school.

"Oh, that? I was wrestling with some of my cousins and fell into a bush. The bush won!" Jessica forced out a fake laugh as she lied to Suzie for the second time in less than five minutes.

RRRRRRRIIIIIIIIINNNNNNNNNNNNGGGGGGGGG G! The tardy bell sounded startling Jessica.

"We need to get to class," Jessica continued. "We can talk more later."

Suzie smiled, "Oh, I have a pass, not a big deal. See ya!"

Making sure she was not going in the same direction as Suzie, she gathered her things and headed for the nearest bathroom. Because Jessica did not have a pass, she knew she'd have to hurry to class and hope for the best. In the restroom Jessica sneaked a peak at her back while she hurriedly changed into her normal school clothes. She had forgotten about hiding her marks. There were still strips of red puffy skin, but not quite as swollen as they were last night. She also noticed a bluish coloration around them now. She'd have to remember to find outfits that did not threaten to reveal her wounds. Ready to go to class she casually walked out of the girls' room. Her class was on the other side of the office so she would have to walk right past it again and hope Mrs. Wright, the principal, wouldn't see her.

Quickening her pace she rounded the corner and started down the hallway where practice had been held. She stopped dead in her tracks.

Outside the office door was the principal. Standing next to Mrs. Wright was a tall lean man dressed in a grease-stained blue shirt and pants. From the looks of him, Jessica guessed he was a mechanic of some kind. To his right was a teenage boy with silky brown hair, the color of dark chocolate. Jessica couldn't see his face, but the resemblance to the boy in her dream was unmistakable. She noticed the older man handing the principal some papers that had been folded up and kept in his front shirt pocket. Jessica couldn't hear what they were saying but guessed that the boy was enrolling in school.

Not wanting to be seen, Jessica stepped back and stood at the end of the trophy case that was against the wall. Finally Mrs. Wright escorted the two down the hall in the other direction. When they were out of sight, Jessica let out a sigh of relief.

She finally made her way to her first hour class by taking the long way around, practically circling the building -- a totally different route then she initially planned. Luckily she made it to her classroom without seeing the principal again. Standing outside the door of her class, Jessica reached down to grab the doorknob. Someone on the inside turned it at the exact same time. They opened the door together. Mrs. Wright stood in front of her with a frown, "Running a little late, Miss Taylor?"

Jessica answered with a mere, "Yes, ma'am."

Mrs. Wright's frown faded as she continued, "I know you have been at school since around 7:00. I hope wherever you have been has been important."

"Yes, ma'am. I was trying to check out some

books from the library and got delayed. I am so sorry," she lied.

"I'm sure you have a pass then." Addressing the teacher inside the classroom, Mrs. Wright said, "Well, Mrs. Willingham I will let you deal with her. Enjoy your day."

Jessica hurried in and scrambled to her seat. Mrs. Willingham smiled and proceeded to write out an assignment on the chalkboard ignoring Jessica's late arrival. As soon as she took out her English notebook, it dawned on her to look around. Sure enough, sitting two rows over was the new student Mrs. Wright had escorted to class. Jessica's body stiffened as she recognized the chocolate brown hair from the hallway. The boy was looking out the window, so Jessica couldn't see his face. All she could see was the side of his cheek. She wondered to herself if he could be the one in her dream. She knew that sounded totally crazy, but she couldn't help entertaining the idea. Even if he did look like the guy in her dream, how would she ever approach him anyway? She might even be wrong; maybe this guy only looked like her dream boy from a distance. Maybe if she saw him up close she would see for sure if it was or wasn't him. If only he would turn around, she would know.

It was as though he read her thoughts. His head turned away from the window to look across the room at all the strange faces. The moment his head turned their eyes met. Instantly, Jessica had her answer.

Chapter 4

The Second Dream

Aaron! Jessica was positive that it was indeed Aaron. Jessica held his eyes as long as she could with her own stare. So many questions whirled around in her head. Did Aaron recognize her as well? Did he know about his presence in her dream? Did he have the same dream last night? Who was he, and how in the world could she have a dream about him one night, and then see him in the flesh at school the next day?

Aaron looked away. He showed no sign of acknowledging Jessica. He looked at her with the same blank expression with which he looked at everyone else. Jessica began to wonder if she had some type of psychic power. She had never really believed in that kind of thing before. A strange feeling came over her.

Minutes before, she was excited to discover that Aaron was sitting two rows away from her in person. Now she was uncertain how to react to such a weird experience. Was she supposed to approach Aaron and say something like, 'Hi, Aaron. My name is Jessica. By the way, did you know I had a dream about you last night?' Or 'Hi, my name is Jessica, but you call me Jesse. Did you happen to have a dream last night with me in it?' Every angle she thought of just seemed awkward plain and simple.

Jessica decided the best thing for her to do was to just sit back and let things work out for themselves. If Aaron wanted to meet her, and if he knew anything about the dream, surely he would say something or give her a sign of some sort. The teacher stood at the front of the room. She was a tall woman with thick, wavy brown hair that daintily brushed her shoulder. She held her English book in her hands with the same loving care that a preacher holds his Bible.

Mrs. Willingham began her lesson with, "I know this has been a hectic morning, but we must get class started. Miss Taylor, Mr. Hernandez, and Miss Cook, I will take care of you three later. I welcome you to our school, Mr. Howser, and hope you make many new friends. If anyone would be so kind to volunteer to help Mr. Howser find his classes today, I am sure he would appreciate it."

Jessica frowned. She didn't know his last name. Because she couldn't quite see him, she became a little frustrated. Mrs. Willingham liked to address everyone as Mr. or Miss. She prided herself in being "proper." Most of the students said they didn't care but deep down inside Jessica really liked it. It made her feel more grown up and respected. A student at the back of the classroom raised his hand.

"I'll help him, Mrs. Willingham."

"Thank you, Mr. Holland," the teacher replied, "We will have a quiz at the end of the hour over your assigned reading, but first I want to cover some things in your book. So everyone open your English books to page 123. "

Jessica's mind wandered. Who was this new person in her English class -- and possibly in her life?

Fifty five minutes crawled by achingly slow. After class when everyone was leaving the room, Jessica joined the exiting crowd. The new student and Mark were only a few people away. Jessica wanted so badly to be closer, but she was near enough to hear their words. Mark was asking him several questions such as where he was from and what his class schedule was. Then he asked something that made Jessica listen carefully for the answer.

"So what is your first name?" Mark inquired.

"A.J." was the boy's simple reply.

Jessica's heart sank for a minute.

"A.J. huh, so does that stand for anything or is that your real name?" Mark pressed.

"It stands for Aaron James. My full name is Aaron James Howser. But I have always gone by A.J." The boy reluctantly answered, as if he hated anyone knowing his real name.

'Yes!' Jessica's heart skipped a beat. She knew it. It was the boy from her dream, but now what?

"Excuse me," Mrs. Willingham's voice interrupted, "three of you need to stay here for a second so I can take care of your tardies."

Jessica exhaled and reluctantly turned around along with the other two students. Aaron walked on out of the classroom and out of Jessica's sight. She stood at Mrs. Willingham's desk awaiting a detention slip. Luckily, Mrs. Willingham was one of those teachers who listened to her students. She simply asked why each of them was late, and each one had an excuse. She let them all off the hook and didn't assign any of them detention -- the usual punishment for tardies.

Day after day Jessica waited for Aaron to give her some sort of sign, anything to show her he knew about the dream. Day after day there was no indication that he knew anything about it. She started thinking that maybe he didn't know about it after all. Maybe it was only in her mind; not his. Besides, she hadn't had any more dreams about him. Jessica feared it was just a weird coincidence, and nothing more. Two weeks crept by, there were no more dreams and no real contact between the two. It was just going to school as usual.

Jessica waited in the background and silently watched him. She noticed that he had begun to make new friends. Unfortunately, she wasn't one of them, and they were nothing like Jessica's friends. The crowd he became part of liked to skip classes, make poor grades, have wild parties on the weekends, and stay outside to smoke cigarettes between classes. It was weird to her, but there was a place on the east side of the high school called "smoker's alley." It wasn't an alley at all. It was just where the kids who smoked hung out and bummed cigarettes off each other. She had heard about that group of kids and how they experimented with different drugs too, mainly marijuana, but she had heard rumors about other things as well. She didn't want to believe he was like that, but, from everything she saw, he was.

Once she passed him in the hallway right after he had been out to smoke and he smelled heavily of whatever cigarette he had been puffing. She remembered thinking that it seemed such a shame, especially because he was so handsome. He had such an athletic build with broad shoulders and narrow hips. His hair was a dark brown that framed his baby blue eyes so well. His skin looked slightly tanned even though it was in the middle of winter. He had long slender legs and stood just slightly bow legged. Jessica thought to herself that, if he came from a family with money, he would probably be the most popular boy in school, but high school kids are ruthless when it comes to accepting new kids. The ones who were star athletes or who came from families with money stood a much better chance of being accepted by everyone. Those who didn't play sports and didn't have money found their selection of potential new friends much smaller.

By this time Jessica had also noticed the way Aaron dressed. When he arrived at school the first day, he was wearing blue jeans, tennis shoes, and an oversized button up shirt that wasn't tucked into his jeans. That seemed quite normal to Jessica at first, but since then he wore the same shoes every day. He wore the shirt several days in a two week period, and he wore the same jeans all the time. Jessica could tell his family must not have very much money at all. With that and having no knowledge of him playing a school sport, Jessica knew he would never be part of her crowd. Not by her choice, but by the unspoken rules of high school social structuring.

She thought about her closest friends at school. They were, on the other hand, the ones whose names filled the honor rolls, were in the student council, wrote for the school newspaper, and were all college-bound. They had all the money they needed, drove the nicest sports cars, wore the most expensive clothing, and were in charge of the school government. Any problems they might have had were kept secret to make everyone else think they had it all. Image was everything.

It became clear that Aaron didn't belong in her world, nor did she belong in his. The excitement that the dream had once brought slowly began to fade. Jessica had hoped that she and Aaron could have enjoyed a wonderful friendship, each knowing each other's deepest thoughts and dreams. She also thought that maybe a close enough relationship could have been formed so that they might even start dating each other. She had hoped her dream was a little more real. She definitely was physically attracted to Aaron. Since he virtually ignored her, she realized that those may have been just silly and useless thoughts.

Friday morning before school, the cheerleading squad practiced to get ready for the special pep rally in honor of the state play-offs. After the practice, Suzie and Jessica ran to the bathroom to fix their hair before going to their first hour class. Ever since the day Suzie had asked Jessica about her back, they had begun to form a closer friendship. To Jessica's surprise, Suzie was much nicer than she seemed at first. She had dreams of a being a successful international business woman. This impressed Jessica because she had no idea what she wanted to be yet. They got along really well. Both of them were friends with everyone and neither had that one special best friend. They were alike in so many ways. Of course, Jessica had friends from childhood who were very dear to her, but for some reason in high school they seemed to go different ways. Suzie was the person with whom she spent most of her time now, and their friendship was definitely growing deeper.

While Jessica was pulling her long blonde hair back into a pony tail, Suzie asked, "So is there anyone you hope to see at the Valentine's dance coming up?

Jessica blushed, "No, not really," she lied.

"Whatever! I can tell by the way you reacted you have your eye on someone," Suzie persisted.

Jessica's mind raced as she tried to figure out if she could trust Suzie.

"Well, there is someone I kind of have a secret crush on, but he doesn't even know I exist," Jessica finally admitted.

"Who?" Suzie squealed in delight. "I can't imagine a single guy in our school who doesn't know you exist. Come on, who is it?"

Jessica had an uneasy feeling, like they weren't alone. She looked under the stall doors for any signs of feet. No one was there.

"Well, let me just say he is like my polar opposite. You would never in a million years guess that I like him. I am not really sure myself why I have a thing for him," she reluctantly continued.

"Do I know him?" Suzie asked as she touched up her eyeliner.

"I don't know. You know what, just pretend I didn't say anything because it is crazy, and there is no chance it would ever work! So tell me who do you want to see?" Jessica tried to deflect the question.

"No way, you are **not** changing the subject on

me that easily. Come on, Jessica, you can tell me. I won't tell anyone." Suzie crossed her heart with her index finger as she pledged silence.

Jessica thought about it for a second. There was a part of her that regretted saying anything at all, and part of her that wanted to spill her guts to Suzie. She decided to take a chance.

"If you will swear that you won't mention this to a single soul, I will tell you. Promise me you won't breathe a word of this to anyone?" Jessica asked, needing to hear Suzie swear her silence once more.

"No problem, I promise not to tell anyone who you like. Of course, if you change your mind and want me to call him and set you up, I will," Suzie promptly replied.

"Ha,ha. Funny." Jessica smirked. She took a deep breath and confessed, "I know you will think this is weird, but I really have this strange attraction to the new guy."

"Which new guy? We get new people at this school all the time," Suzie complained. "Narrow it down just a little, will ya?"

"Ummm. A.J. Howser." Jessica finally revealed his name.

Suzie crinkled up her nose, "What do you possibly see in him?"

Before she could say anything more, they heard feet hit the ground with a loud thud. Apparently, someone had been standing on a toilet and jumped to the floor. A bathroom stall door slammed open. Out stormed Ronda Reed, the high school's toughest girl. She was a rather puny looking girl, standing no taller than five feet and weighing a whopping 90 lbs. No one messed with her because she was as mean as wolverine. She got into fights weekly. She didn't care if you were male or female; she could pick a fight with anyone who made her mad and would somehow always find a way to win.

Ronda's deep voice pierced the air, "Which one of you stuck up little bitches likes my A.J.? He is MY boyfriend! You better back off and leave him alone!"

Ronda was apparently planning on skipping class and hiding out in the bathroom. Jessica swallowed. It was just her luck. Jessica and Suzie both took a step back.

Ronda stepped toward them and continued, "That's what I thought, neither of you can stand up to me." She pushed Jessica. Jessica took a couple steps back but didn't respond. She then turned her attention to Suzie and gave her the same kind of push she just gave Jessica. Suzie, too, stepped back to keep her balance but did not respond either.

"If either of you try to talk to him in any way I will hunt you down and kick your little cheerleading ass. No, I will kick both of your asses! Understood?"

Both cheerleaders stood in a silent, fearful daze, and nodded their heads. Ronda marched out of the bathroom. When they were sure she was gone, Jessica and Suzie agreed calling him would be a life threatening mistake. Jessica went on to class convinced that she should forget about ever talking to Aaron. Ever! Why was this so hard?

When Jessica entered her first hour class, she

was a little depressed about what had just happened. First of all, she was terrified of Ronda, and, secondly, she realized that Aaron already had a girlfriend. That complicated things in her mind even more. What did he see in Ronda of all people? Jessica took her seat and stared out the window.

Aaron waltzed in the room as the tardy bell rang and casually took his seat. Jessica wondered what it would be like to be his girlfriend. She had never gone out with a guy like him before. In fact, she had only had three different boyfriends her entire life. All of them had money. All of them were athletes. All of them had plans to go to college. All of them were opposite of Aaron.

Jessica's parents wanted her to concentrate on her school work, not boys anyway. They wanted her to graduate high school with a perfect grade point average so it would increase her chances of getting academic scholarships to good colleges. So when the topic of boys ever came up, they would lecture her about her priorities in life.

Suddenly, Jessica's thoughts were interrupted as she heard a pencil hit the floor. She looked down to see it had rolled under her desk. Jessica reached down and picked it up. When she returned to an upright position, she glanced around to see to whom it belonged. To her astonishment, Aaron was looking directly at her. She held the pencil up in a gesture as if to ask, 'Is this yours?'

Aaron answered with a nod. Jessica extended her arm offering the pencil to him. He stood up and leaned over the desk that separated them. Reaching for the pencil, Aaron's hand slightly touched Jessica's. A shiver went down her spine.

Aaron whispered, "Thanks, Jesse," and returned to his seat.

Jessica was frozen; he just called her 'Jesse.' Was this the sign she had been waiting for? He actually knew her name. Of course, he had been at school for a couple of weeks and could have heard others say her name. No wait! She went by Jessica at school. He knew her name was Jesse! He knew it.

Jessica became lost in her own thoughts and daydreamed about the handsome young boy through the rest of class. Only the dismissal bell ringing brought her back to reality.

***

Loud, obnoxious shouts and laughter and the shuffle of feet indicated to the cheerleaders, preparing behind the curtain for the rally, that the rest of the student body had arrived in the auditorium. Everyone was excited about the basketball play-offs! It had been years since their team had done very well, and they all felt this could be their year to win state. Excitement flooded the air.

The cheerleaders took their places on stage. As the curtain opened, a roar from the student body erupted. Music flooded the auditorium from the band playing the school's fight song. Soon, the cheerleaders joined in with their dance routine. Choreographed cheers combined with the electrifying noise created a deafening, raw, primal excitement that permeated the air.

Standing on stage, Jessica could see out across the entire auditorium. She could see the seniors lining the front rows with the junior class right behind them. Some of the sophomores were pushed to the back on the ground floor and the rest of them were seated up in the balcony. Jessica's eyes roamed seat to seat, row to row searching for Aaron. She was haunted by Ronda's words, but she knew she had never attempted to contact Aaron so Ronda couldn't do anything to her. There was no harm in looking for him in a pep assembly.

Finally she spotted him on the very back row on the ground floor. Next to him were some really rough looking guys and then Ronda. The whole row of them appeared to care little about the pep rally, as if they wanted to be anywhere else but stuck in the auditorium. Ronda sat with her arms folded across her chest. Aaron stared off into space.

Cheer after cheer, the pep assembly went on. The auditorium shook with screams, whistles, and the stomping of feet when the principal called the head basketball coach to the stage. He gave a warm greeting to the crowd then started introducing the athletes that made up the boys' basketball team. For each name announced, a tall lanky boy came running up on stage in full uniform. The cheerleaders stood to the side and performed a jump or some other gymnastic move to show their spirited support for each player. Everything seemed to be going as planned, and Jessica was really enjoying herself.

Between jumps, Jessica looked out across the audience. She located Aaron once again. She was shocked to see that Mrs. Wright, the principal, had made her way to the back row and was motioning for someone to follow her. Aaron stood with his arms folded across his chest. He reluctantly squeezed his way to the end of the back row.

Jessica hoped that Aaron wasn't in trouble. Another movement from the back doorway caught Jessica's eye. Aaron's dad stood rigidly. Jessica recognized him from the day she saw Aaron enrolling.

Another name was called out by the coach. Jessica had been paying so much attention to the situation in the back that she almost didn't jump. Luckily, Suzie's shouts prompted her to join in just in time. Her body went through the motions, but her mind was focused on what was happening to Aaron.

Mrs. Wright pointed to the doorway as if telling him he needed to leave with his father. Mrs. Wright then walked on, monitoring the rest of the crowd. Aaron slowly approached his father. Jessica wasn't sure, but she sensed something wasn't right. As soon as Aaron entered the hallway, Jessica could see his father grab him by the shirt and jerk him out of her sight. Jessica had seen this behavior before by her own father but never with anyone else's, especially not in public.

Suzie elbowed Jessica, "Come on you need to keep cheering. I know who you are watching and you have to let it go."

Jessica glanced at her then smiled a sad smile. She forced herself to be the spirited little cheerleader she was expected to be. She was both exhausted and relieved when the pep assembly came to an end.

On her drive home, she turned her radio up until the bass vibrated the speakers. She had about two hours before she needed to be at the basketball game. The images of Aaron filled her mind. Jessica wished she had the nerve to call him. She wanted to know that he was all right. Then the memory of Ronda filled her head, and she knew Ronda would stay true to her word if she found out Jessica called him. She decided she had better not. Even though she knew it was probably not a good idea, she that she might work up the nerve to ask him about it at the game.

She pulled her car into the driveway and shut it off. Jessica sat in the car a second as the image of AJ's father jerking him around played like a movie in her head. She closed her eyes and forced herself into motion. Jessica didn't even notice the crisp air as she headed into the house.

Her mother was in the kitchen and called out a greeting, "Hello Jesse, you are home early. I thought you had a basketball game to cheer at today."

Jessica gave her mother a hug and replied, "The game isn't until later tonight. I thought I would slip in a quick nap because I have been so tired all day today."

Her mother asked if she needed to wake her at a certain time. Jessica agreed that was a good idea so she wouldn't have to set an alarm clock. She left the room to go lie down.

Her concerns about Aaron stayed with her as her eyes grew heavy. It wasn't long before sleep claimed her body and a dream filled her mind.

Aaron was sitting at a picnic table looking off into space facing away from Jessica. She recognized the park. They had met here in the last dream. She tiptoed up behind him. Quietly, Jessica lifted her arms and cupped her hands over both Aaron's eyes. She playfully asked, "Guess who?"

Aaron responded with a slight flinch, then a quiet voice asked, "Jesse, is that you?"

"Yep, how'd you know?" Jessica giggled then walked around the other side of the picnic table to seat herself across from him. Aaron's head looked down at the table. Jessica continued, "So how is it going?"

Aaron looked up for the first time. His right eye and right cheek were covered with a massive bruise. Jessica gasped in horror. She started to ask him what happened, but, as their eyes met, Jessica was able to see things she had never seen before. It was as though she was dreaming within a dream, and she could see Aaron's memories deep in her own mind. She instantly knew so much more about him. She could see he loved cars and motorcycles. That he had a very large Hot Wheels collection from when he was a child. She could see he also had a grandmother that was dear to him, but she had passed away not long ago. She could see his favorite color was black. She could see how Aaron secretly would watch his mother crying in her bedroom and not know how to comfort her. Then she saw how he had gotten the black eye. His father, who was a larger version of Aaron, had punched him with his fist after what appeared to be an argument dealing with a car. The car looked to be a classic of some kind. She continued to watch as Aaron fell to the ground, his eye swelling rapidly and blood dripping from his nose. He sat there blotting his blood with his sleeve while glaring at his father with an ice cold stare. His father's top lip curled up in a snarl, and his teeth were locked together. He was breathing hard as his anger surged through his veins. After the attack his father stormed off in a rage that was all too familiar.

Jessica immediately apologized to Aaron, "I am so sorry. He had no right to treat you that way."

She stood up and joined him on his side of the picnic table. Jessica reached up to put her arm around his shoulder in an effort to comfort him.

"Could you see it? Was it just like I saw into your mind our last time here together?" Aaron asked.

"I could. It was as though I was thinking the thoughts myself, but they were your thoughts and your memories. The one thing I didn't see was why your father was angry about that car," Jessica replied.

Aaron offered more details, "I scratched his race car with one of the screwdrivers I was using when I was working on the engine. It was an accident; I simply dropped it and it left a scratch in the paint. I forgot to tell him about it and obviously he found it while I was at school. "

"It's not right. It is not right how parents can act however they want to act, no matter who it hurts. I wish there was a way to stop them," Jessica railed.

"Everyone has his own problems. No one has an easy life. We just have to learn to cope with the problems we have been dealt," Aaron *replied.*

He seemed so much more calm and analytical than Jessica. She was just angry; angry at everyone, except Aaron.

"Does your dad do this a lot?" Jessica asked quietly.

Aaron thought a moment, "Not a whole lot. I just never know when he's going to snap. The day I'm bigger than he is will be the day it stops though."

"Have you thought about reporting him to the police?" Jessica wondered out loud.

"Yeah, I've thought about it. I just don't know what would happen if I did. I'm not willing to chance it. I can take it. It only hurts for a little while. Plus, it makes me tougher," Aaron justified.

Jessica changed the subject, "The last time we met you said you had been waiting 17 years for that day. What did you mean by that?"

Aaron smiled. His tanned skin made his teeth look even whiter. Jessica loved that smile. It warmed her heart, every chamber of it.

"Well, do you ever get the feeling that we have known each other forever?" he asked in reply.

Jessica thought a moment then started to feel a tugging sensation. Something was pulling her out of the park. It was forcing her away against her own will. She reached out and hugged Aaron before she spoke. She wanted whatever was tugging at her to go away. Maybe if she held him she could stay. He felt so warm and so good. She didn't want to leave at all but an invisible force was pulling at her again -- harder and harder every second. It was a jerking her now.

"Aaron, I have to go now, but I do feel that way? I want to talk more about this. I'm sorry to leave. We will see each other again won't we? I need to see you..."

"Jesse, wake up! If you don't wake up you will be late! Jesse! Jesse!" her mother's high pitched voice squealed as she tugged on Jessica's arm. Leaving Aaron behind, Jessica had been pulled into reality.

"I'm awake, mom. Thanks," Jessica resentfully replied.

As her mother walked out of the room, Jessica muttered in sarcasm, "Thanks a lot."

Chapter 5

The Necklace

Jessica drove in a daze to the basketball game. Suzie met her at the front entrance, "Hey, girl! You ready for tonight's game?"

Jessica nodded her head and smiled. She really wanted to tell Suzie about the dreams, but now was not the time. They walked together into the gym and started setting up. Suzie asked Jessica if her bow was tied in a pretty way or if it looked sloppy. Jessica thought it needed to be a little neater so she untied it and carefully tied Suzie a new bow. Then Suzie looked at Jessica's ponytail and offered to do the same. Jessica had hurriedly put her hair back so was happy to let Suzie redo her pony-tail and bow. Both girls said their "hellos" to the other cheerleaders arriving and ran to the restroom to touch up their make-up.

"Suzie, will you do me a favor tonight?" Jessica asked once they were inside the girls' restroom.

"Why, sure!"

Jessica smiled. She knew they were the first ones in the restroom since they had to turn on the lights so she wasn't worried about being overheard like last time. "Will you help me watch for A.J. Howser? I really need to talk to him."

"Jessica! Are you out of your mind? Do you have any memory whatsoever of Ronda Reed?"

"I know, I know. This is about something in our first hour class we have together," Jessica lied.

Suzie squinted her eyes and took a deep breath. "Okay," she said reluctantly, "but you better not do anything to get our asses kicked! You know I'm a pacifist!"

Jessica laughed, "So a pacifist, huh? Sure! I promise to be super careful so Ronda doesn't even know."

"So do you still have a thing for him?"

Jessica hesitated and thought about how to answer her. "Let's just say I am very aware that we are from two different worlds and have nothing in common. I still think he is extremely good-looking, but he's not my type. Ronda can have him." As soon as she said that, she felt a pang of jealously in her gut. It hurt to say that out loud. She really didn't know why she had a thing for him. After all, their only true interactions were in two dreams she had had. Jessica was definitely conflicted.

The two girls finished dabbing on more blush and applying new lip gloss over their lipstick then ran out to the gym to join the rest of the squad.

Throughout the entire game, Jessica searched the stands for any sign of Aaron. She wanted to know if her dream was true. Had Aaron's father given him a black eye? She didn't see him. The game seemed to go on forever. It didn't even matter that her team had won, and they were having the best season they had had in 20 years. All that seemed to matter is that she needed to somehow make contact with Aaron without Ronda knowing about it. She needed to find out if her dream was accurate.

That night when she went home she had a hard time falling asleep. She tossed and turned trying to stop thinking of Aaron. The harder she tried to stop, the more she seemed to think of him. She hoped that her thoughts would lead to another dream, but they didn't.

Saturday rolled around. Jessica had tennis lessons in the morning then studied for another anatomy test in the early afternoon. Later she went to the mall for a couple of hours with Suzie. She still kept wondering about Aaron, but shopping with Suzie was a lot of fun. They bopped around to different trendy stores and tried on several outfits. They visited shoes stores, jewelry stores, toy stores, and the mall's food court. The best store of all, though, was Miss Shawntal's Boutique. It had every kind of accessory a girl could want. There were scarves, purses, jewelry, hats, belts, wallets, watches, sunglasses, socks, and shoes. They spent at least an hour in that one store laughing and looking at every isle and every display. Once her shopping budget had run out, she and Suzie decided to call it a night. Each girl had driven her own car since they were coming from different sides of town. Suzie drove a red 1982 Mazda RX7 which suited her flashy personality. As she loaded her shopping bags she playfully blew Jessica a kiss and waved good-bye.

Jessica threw her bags of new clothes and accessories onto her passenger seat. Her mind kept wandering back to Aaron. Instead of driving home she started her Corvette and took off in the opposite direction of Suzie. Jessica decided to drive around to check the local hangouts. Maybe Aaron was out and about and they could "accidentally" run into each other. No luck. She thought she saw one of his friend's cars at the local arcade. Perfect, that would give her a reason to go in and look. So she parked, went in, and walked around for a while, but she never saw Aaron. She saw Darren, who had grown up just down the street from her, but no Aaron. She went up to Darren and made small talk so she wouldn't look silly for leaving so abruptly. He was nice, very much like the brother she had never had, but there wasn't much to say. She lied and said she was looking for Suzie. He seemed fine with that explanation and after a few minutes Jessica left.

Sunday rolled around and Jessica mechanically dressed for church. Her family went to a nondenominational church. Supposedly, her parents attended that church because they were open minded; however, Jessica felt like they only went there because it was the "cool" church to attend in town. Most of the wealthier people went there, and it seemed to be more about bragging rights than anything else. Jessica really struggled with going because both her mother and her father went, too. She never could understand how one could go to church on Sunday yet drink and beat his daughter other days of the week. Jessica believed in God so she hoped that God would take care of him someday for acting like he was a good Christian man to the world, but his actions were less than Godly. It just felt like one big acting job.

After church she ran home, grabbed a sandwich, and decided to drive around town again, just in case she could catch a glimpse of Aaron.

Again he was nowhere to be found. Her obsession with him seemed to be growing. She just wished she could see him to confirm what she saw in her dream.

Since the first day Aaron arrived at school, Jessica had been having a hard time concentrating on her homework. She had always made straight "A's" and never dreamed she would ever have any difficulty maintaining that. Unfortunately, she spent the entire weekend obsessing over Aaron instead of studying. Not until Monday morning did she realize that she should have been doing more than just looking for Aaron. She should have studied for her anatomy class and completed a journal writing activity for her English class.

Jessica ran to her first hour class pleading with Mrs. Willingham to let her have just one more day to turn it in. The teacher listened patiently to her excuse. Jessica claimed that she didn't have time to finish it because she had been out of town for the weekend. Jessica knew she was lying, but she was desperate. She couldn't take a zero or it would bring her grade down. One time, her father actually scolded her for having an "A minus."

As soon as she finished her explanation, Mrs. Willingham smiled and said in a matter-of-fact-voice, "Miss Taylor, I reminded the entire class on Thursday and Friday of last week that those journals were due today with no exceptions. I also explained that, if you had other obligations over the weekend, you should complete the journal on Friday. I feel certain that plenty of time was provided for you to have finished it, long before today's deadline. I am sorry that you didn't take my advice, but the paper is due by class time today. I have never accepted late work, and I am not going to start now. Your grade is high enough that this one zero should not take you below a "B."

Jessica couldn't believe her ears, a "B"? She had never in her life made a "B." Her father would go through the roof! She hoped that she could talk Mrs. Willingham into allowing her to turn in extra credit to keep her "A," but now was not the time to do that. If she tried to speak, she was sure the only thing that would come out of her would be a whimper which would inevitably turn into a cry. She turned around, put her hand up to her forehead, and took her seat. She immediately laid her head down on her folded arms. Her whole world seemed to falling apart. She couldn't believe she was about to receive her first zero on a homework assignment in a class that didn't accept late work. What a stupid rule! What a stupid rule, indeed.

Jessica was so upset that she didn't notice Aaron striding in to take his seat as the tardy bell rang. Mrs. Willingham started the class by taking up the weekend journals. When Jessica was sure she could raise her head without bawling, she did. She had never experienced what it was like not to have her homework completed. Now she knew. To her it felt awful, as though everyone else in the room was smart and she was dumb. No, not just stupid – she felt like a failure. A dumb, stupid, failure, that's what she was. She was sure her father would agree.

When Jessica realized that Aaron was there, she forgot about the homework assignment for a moment and a glimmer of hope filled her body. She could finally tell if there was truth to her dream after all. Jessica sat on the edge of her chair trying to catch a glimpse of his face. Aaron was staring out the window, something he did a lot. Jessica could only see the back of his head and one of his ears. She stretched a little further. If only he would look to the left, she would know.

"I want all eyes to the front. Our lesson is going to be a difficult one today, and it would be most helpful if some of you would pay attention," Mrs. Willingham's authoritative voice jerked Jessica's attention to the front of the classroom.

As she cleared her voice, Mrs. Willingham glared right at Jessica. Jessica felt a flush of red come over her face. She swallowed hard and took a deep breath. Shifting her weight back toward the center of her chair, she sat up straight to show her teacher she was ready to listen. Mrs. Willingham turned around to write something on the board.

Jessica's eyes found their way back over to Aaron. He, too, was facing the front now. Jessica could see the side of his cheek. She couldn't tell if there was anything different about him; if only he would turn to his left more. Unexpectedly, the pencil he was jiggling in his hand slipped away from him and clicked as it hit the floor. Jessica couldn't have asked for anything better. When Aaron bent over to get it he turned toward her, there was no imagining it; Aaron had a strip of purplish-green that swept under one eye. Jessica's heart skipped a beat. She was hoping he would look at her directly, but he didn't. He simply picked up his pencil and returned his stare to the front of the room. Excitement flooded her soul to know her dream was real. She was thankful he had a hard time keeping hold of his pencils. Then a wave of sadness hit her, not for herself, but for Aaron.

Then her emotion changed again. It was confusion. Something very, very weird was going on. She was dreaming of a person with whom she had never even had a conversation before. She dreamed of him BEFORE she even met him. Why was she dreaming of him? Was he dreaming of her too? Jessica started wondering again if she were psychic. She had always thought those types of people were fake and lied about all that kind of stuff. Now she wasn't so sure. Not knowing what to say or how to react, she sat quietly through classes the rest of the day, and barely spoke to anyone, even Suzie. She had to figure out a way to see if Aaron knew anything about the dreams.

That night Jessica didn't dream and woke up disappointed. She went to school as usual. Nothing spectacular happened. The only highlight was in first hour. Aaron looked her way and actually smiled at her. His bright blue eyes and pearly white smile melted her heart every time. Though his clothes were nothing but rags, Jessica had a deep attraction to him that came from the soul. He was nothing like any of her friends, nor was he anything like the person she dreamed she would marry someday; but there was a chemistry so strong she couldn't deny it. The desire to be near him was getting stronger every day.

Friday finally rolled around after an uneventful week. Jessica went home after school and plopped her backpack full of books down on the kitchen table. She went into the den to watch television for a few minutes before starting on her homework. She was so involved in her show she didn't hear the front door bang open. The volume was up high, and it drowned out the approaching footsteps that stomped down the hallway. Her hand froze, grasping the remote control when the roar of her father's voice pierced the room, "What in the hell is the meaning of this?"

Her head jerked around to see what he was yelling about. In his hand he clutched a pink piece of paper. It looked like a half sheet of paper or a form of some kind. Confused, Jessica tried to make sense of what was making him so angry. She knew her father shouldn't be home yet. He usually didn't get home until after five o'clock. It was only three thirty. He was no longer dressed in his suit and tie. He still was wearing his dress shirt, unbuttoned at the sleeves which loosely hung around his wrists. Jessica noticed the very familiar smell of alcohol. Jessica knew she needed to be very careful about what she said. If her father had been drinking, he had very little patience.

"This is a notice from your school. Mrs. Willingham says she is concerned about you." His hands trembled with anger as he held the letter up to read again.

"Your English teacher says you didn't turn in some 'weekend journal' assignment that was due Monday and that your mind has been wandering in her class," her father continued. "Can you explain all of this? She is afraid your 'A' will fall to a 'B' and could possibly fall to a 'C' if you keep this up."

Jessica had no idea her teacher would send something home. Why didn't Mrs. Willingham just talk to her? She tried to think of some logical explanation for everything. Nothing came to mind. All she could think of was not saying something that would get her into more trouble.

"I don't know what she is talking about. I thought I turned that in. It must be a mistake. She must have lost it," Jessica said the only thing that came to her mind.

She knew it was a weak response, but she couldn't tell him the truth. He would never ever understand her preoccupation with Aaron and the dreams she had lately. She watched him as the color of his face changed from an irritated pink to an enraged fiery red. She knew he was losing his temper. She found herself backing away from him.

Mr. Taylor hissed, "This is not good enough! I am not going to sit back and watch you while you ruin your perfect grade point average. Do you realize this could ruin your chances at Valedictorian? Not to mention the thousands of dollars down the drain in scholarship money. How could you do something so stupid? How could you? I have worked my ass off to give you this life. But you don't care, do you? Your only job is to make good grades. That's it! You have it so easy compared to other kids. Do you know I had to work from the time I was 15 years old? Nobody paid my way. I am supporting your ass so you can do something with your life and this is the thanks I get?! You just want to throw it all away. You repulse me! Do you hear me? Look at me when I am talking to you!"

Jessica had been looking down to avoid the stress she felt when he was this way. She started to look up but apparently wasn't fast enough and it enraged Mr. Taylor. "You disrespectful little..." he snapped.

The raw emotion he felt inside was unleashed on Jessica. He lunged at her and grabbed her by the upper part of her arms. His hands tightly squeezed them as he shook her with every word he spat. Then using all his strength, he threw her up against the wall. She hit with a loud bang. Pain exploded inside her head where it smashed into the wall, and everything went black for a moment. She collapsed to her knees. Her hands involuntarily reached for her throbbing head before she fell the rest of the way to the ground. Motionless she lay moaning in pain.

Mr. Taylor stepped forward. His breathing was deep and somewhat loud. He clenched his teeth, held his hand high in the air as though he were going to slap her but there was no clear shot to her face.

"You know what? You're not even worth it. I don't know why I gave you my last name. It sure as hell wasn't for you to disgrace it!" Then he lowered his hand just as quickly.

Through clenched teeth he hissed his final words, "You better get your act together."

Jessica didn't dare meet his gaze. She remained still while Mr. Taylor stormed out of the room. As he passed her, he took a foot and kicked her legs out his way. Jessica laid her head on the cold wooden floor. She worried that one day he wouldn't hold back. For now he was smart enough not to leave marks that could be easily seen by others. She didn't know if that would always be the case. All she knew was she couldn't wait until she was eighteen. The day she turned eighteen would be the day she moved out of his house forever.

Jessica's mother arrived home shortly after the attack to find her still lying on the floor in a light sleep. Clearly under the influence of alcohol,

Mr. Taylor had collapsed on the sofa in the next room. Jessica's mom gently lifted her daughter to a sitting position while talking softly to her. Her mother knew about her father's violent temper but was powerless against him. For now she just cleaned Jessica up with a damp cloth. She went into the kitchen to get a bag of ice for Jessica's head. The impact of hitting the wall left a knot and a small cut on the back of Jessica's head. The blood had dried in her hair making it clump together in the back.

"I'm sorry, honey. I should have known this was going to happen. He called me at work around lunchtime. Apparently he had come home to eat and checked the mail. By the looks of his condition, he must have taken the rest of the afternoon off and spent it drinking," Mrs. Taylor apologized.

Jessica was just glad her mother was there with her. She knew her father would leave her alone if her mother were there.

"Let's go to your bedroom. I will bring supper to you there. The best thing for you to do is to avoid your father the rest of the night. I don't want any more confrontations. I will try to talk to him more when he's awake. Was this about your teacher's note? He told me a little about it," Mrs. Taylor asked, trying to understand her husband's violent reaction.

"Yes. I don't want to talk about it now. I promise I will explain later, Mom," Jessica replied, her head still pounding with pain.

Jessica crawled into her bed. Tears pooled in the corners of her eyes, and then like a dam giving way, became streams that flowed down her cheeks to stain her pillow. She never understood why the tears always came after the physical pain. She questioned why her mother married such a jerk. And, if he hated her so much, why did he even talk to her? She hated him, too. She hated what he did to her and how he made her feel.

Jessica's mother brought her supper and some aspirin for her headache. Jessica wondered if she had a concussion. Her mother said if she did, the signs of it may not show up until later. Jessica sat back and heartily ate her mother's homemade soup which was leftover from the night before. The warm meal somehow calmed her nerves. Her mother left the room.

Feeling satisfied, she put the empty bowl on a tray that was on her night stand, rolled over and fell into a deep sleep. She woke up about an hour later to find her mother had removed the tray and turned off the lights. She fluffed her pillow and lay her head back down. Thoughts whirled around in her mind even as her body gave into sleep. The next thing she knew Jessica was in a dream.

Walking along a sandy beach in the evening, watching the sun as it hung low, she rolled up her jeans to her knees to enjoy the occasional splash of the waves. Aaron was sitting on a large rock looking out at the endless ocean waves. His bruise was gone. He looked up and smiled when he saw Jessica approaching. Her walk turned into a playful run to meet him. When she reached the rock, Aaron jumped down to the ground and took her hands in his. He looked into her eyes allowing her thoughts to be his own. Both knew he was seeing her memories. A frown replaced his smile as he watched the events of the evening unfold in her mind.

"I'm sorry, Jesse. You don't deserve that. No one does. It is not right of him to act that way just to make a point. It hurts me to know what he does to you," he whispered softly.

"It's okay, I'll survive. I always do, and I think I'm stronger for it as well. Plus, as soon as I'm eighteen I will move out of there," Jessica replied, trying to comfort him.

"Do you really think that is the best answer? To just wait it out? He could really hurt you one of these days. I think you should tell someone that can make him stop, like the school counselor, a teacher, or the police," Aaron told her.

"Aaron, I'll be fine. I don't want to cause a scene. I don't want anyone to know. It would be too embarrassing." Jessica confided in him.

"Really? You think you can last another year and a half? I think you should tell Mrs. Ford, the counselor. She can at least give you advice on what to do." Aaron persisted.

Jessica thought about what he said and then replied, "If telling Mrs. Ford is such a good idea, why haven't you done it?"

"It's different with a guy. Guys are supposed to be tough. Plus, I'm new at this school. I know there are adults out there you can trust. You just have to look in the right places," Aaron shared his philosophy.

Jessica responded quickly, "Wait, you want me to get help but you won't do anything to help yourself. That doesn't make much sense."

"Jesse, all I know is that I want to be here to help you. I don't know what to do. I just want it to stop. If that means telling someone, then I am all for it. But if you don't want to, I won't pressure you either. Come here." He motioned to the rock he had been sitting on.

The cool breeze that sailed above the water lightly danced around their faces. It felt so clean and refreshing. With Aaron's help Jessica managed to climb up on the rock that was almost as tall as she was. Aaron hoisted himself up to join her.

"I love it here. I wish we could stay here forever," Jessica smiled.

Aaron maintained his serious tone, "Look, Jesse, I'm not here to judge you or tell you what to do. I do have to tell you, though, that I am confused about our relationship. At school, you act like you don't even know me. Yet, when I meet you here in our dreams, you are everything I have ever wanted in my life. You are beautiful, smart, and you understand me in a way no one else does. It is perfect in our dreams but not in real life. I have so many feelings. I can't make sense of them all."

Jessica was stunned to hear him open up so much. She felt exactly the same way.

"I am very confused, too. I thought it was you who was ignoring me. I have always wanted to be near you since the first day you came to school, but Ronda put a stop to that real fast. Since she IS your girlfriend, how can you say those things to me? I don't get that at all," Jessica replied.

"I wish I could explain it. I'll try, but I don't know if it will come out the way I mean it. Ronda is someone who is similar to me. She doesn't have money either. She really is more like a sister. At school, she is the kind of person other people would expect me to be with. She is funny, and most of the time I like her company. On the other hand, my heart really belongs to you, but you are someone I can't have. It's like we come from the same place but we live in different worlds. I have thought about how we could be together, but I haven't figured out a solution. All I know is I can't get you out of my mind. You are the one I think about all the time, not Ronda," Aaron confessed.

"Oh, Aaron, I didn't know you felt that way. You are all I seem to think about, too. It is so complicated. You are constantly in my thoughts, but I can't tell anyone because nobody would really understand. Suzie knows I find you attractive, but that's it. My preoccupation with you is even affecting my school work. I have never felt this way before. I've never had dreams of someone like this before. It's exciting and scary at the same time," Jessica acknowledged.

"I'm so glad you feel that way, too. I have thought about you nonstop since our first dream but don't know how to talk to you in real life. I brought you something, Jesse. I *want you to have this as a reminder of what I said. No matter what happens, you are the one who has my heart!" Aaron explained as he pulled a long dainty chain out of his pocket.*

On the end of the chain, a cross gracefully hung. He placed it in her hands. Jessica held the necklace up and looked at it. It was the most beautiful and unique thing she had ever seen. The cross was a series of wires that were interwoven. Then in different places throughout there were tiny little ball-like structures. Inside those balls were suspended hearts. One had to really look carefully at it to see how amazing it was. From a distance it looked like a cross. Up close it was very complex in its design and so much more than just a cross. It was very fitting for the situation at hand.

She immediately hugged him and whispered, "Thank you so much."

"Turn around and I will put it on you. I meant everything I said, Jesse. No matter what happens at school, you are the one I truly want."

As soon as he fastened the necklace, Jessica turned around to face him. Aaron pulled her close to him and softly pressed his lips to hers.

The kiss sent electricity through Jessica's body. She knew Aaron was telling the truth. She knew beyond a shadow of a doubt that this was the one with whom she was to spend her life. Having Aaron's arms around her felt so good. She felt so safe, so loved.

As their lips parted, she looked into Aaron's beautiful baby blue eyes. He smiled at her and kissed her again. As their lips parted the second time, Aaron softly whispered, "It's time for me to go. We will be together here and in real life one day. I know it."

Jessica took a deep breath of fresh air. She wanted to stay in that moment with him forever, but she knew he needed to leave. "I want that more than anything, Aaron. No matter what happens at school, I want that too!"

The ocean began to fade as did Aaron's handsome face.

Jessica rolled over to look at her clock. It read 2:00 AM. She looked around the darkened room, confirming that she was at home in her bed. She didn't want to be there; she wanted to be back at the beach with Aaron. She tried closing her eyes and going back to sleep. She wanted somehow to get back to that beautiful beach. She wanted to be back in Aaron's arms. Jessica sighed and was unable to go back to sleep no matter how hard she tried.

Suddenly she remembered the necklace that Aaron had given her in the dream. She raised her right hand up to her throat. Hoping to feel the necklace, she only felt her bare skin and the disappointment of not finding anything. She lowered her fingertips a little, gently searching, hoping to find a trace of a necklace. Her finger surprisingly caught on a chain that was loosely fastened around her neck. Disappointment turned to astonishment and then joy. Her fingers slid down the chain to rest on the cross.

Jesse jumped out of bed and ran into her bathroom. She flipped on the light and ran to the mirror. It was the one that was in the dream all right. Something very strange, but very wonderful, was going on, and it was a little disconcerting. Jessica knew she had to speak to Aaron in person, and soon. She decided that, first thing in the morning, she would drive over to Aaron's house and ask him about the necklace. It seemed a little crazy, but she had to know that this was for real. She had to know if he was sharing the dreams or if her mind was creating this fantasy world that would never come true.

Chapter 6

Hidden Park

Saturday morning couldn't arrive soon enough. Jessica woke up as soon as the sun peered in through the curtains. Her room was so beautiful in the mornings. She had a large east-facing window that welcomed every sunrise. Pastel yellow curtains that framed the windows lit up when the sunlight poured in through the window panes. Today they came alive as the brightness of a new day flooded the room.

Jessica quickly dressed and pulled her long blonde hair into a ponytail like she did most days. She had showered sometime after eating the soup last night, but she didn't remember exactly when. Last night was such a blur, except for the dream. She put on a touch of make-up. She first put on a light foundation since she had such a fair complexion. Then she took her black eyeliner and traced the shape of her eyes. She followed it up with a touch of purple eye shadow. She dabbed the shadow just where the eyeliner was. Purple seemed to bring out the blue in her eyes. Looking at her eyes made her daydream for a second; if she and Aaron had children together they would absolutely have blue eyes. Hers were light blue in the middle with a dark blue ring around the outer part of the iris. She finished up with black mascara on the tips of her eyelashes. She felt lucky in that area. Her eyelashes were long so she only had to put mascara on the tips to make them look right. She finished putting on her make-up by coating her lips with a slightly tinted lip gloss. She wanted to feel confident for what she was about to do, and putting on make-up seemed to help.

Though she was sore from her father's attack, she was revitalized with an anxious hope. She had been having such strong feelings for Aaron -- feelings that strengthened with each dream. Thinking they were only images in her own mind, she never had the courage to approach Aaron before. Now wearing the necklace helped her realize that her dreams were more than just mere images of fantasy. Their relationship was real – somehow – somewhere -- it was real. She was wearing the proof.

Getting out of the house unnoticed was an extremely simple task. Jessica's father was sure to sleep until noon with a hangover. Her mother didn't get up until midmorning, just soon enough to join her ladies' group at the country club for a round of golf. Their tee time was always at eleven a.m. Jessica jumped into her 1983 convertible Corvette. Her father had bought it for her brand new on her sixteenth birthday. Jessica got to pick out the color, and she chose the one that looked like it was black from a distance, but in a certain light, you could see it was really a dark blue.

It was unseasonably warm for winter, but that was typical for Oklahoma. It was so warm she let the top down. As she backed out of her driveway onto the street, the cool morning breeze brushed over the top of her head.

She had never officially been to Aaron's house before, but once after school she saw him driving away in an old green car. She couldn't even identify the make and model, but suspected it was really old. Since she didn't have to be anywhere in particular she followed him from a distance. She watched as he drove through an older neighborhood with small houses. As soon as she saw him pull into a drive way, she turned off on another road. Much later she returned to find his car was still parked in the grass, alongside another car. She felt pretty confident that was where he lived; however, not 100% positive. She decided to trust her gut and drive there again.

About 10 minutes into her drive, Jessica realized she hadn't eaten breakfast and was a little hungry. She found the nearest convenience store and bought a box of assorted doughnuts and two half-pints of chocolate milk. She knew it wasn't very nutritious, but her parents wouldn't know, and, since she didn't have tennis lessons, she figured she could survive without the nourishment.

Jessica pulled into the small neighborhood. She looked around at all the houses and cars parked by them. She took it all in. The lawns were not well manicured as they were in her neighborhood. She didn't notice any Audis, Mercedes, Jaguars, or BMW's. Many of the houses had dogs barking behind tall wooden fences that surrounded their back yards. Children's forgotten toys scattered across front lawns, rotting from exposure to the weather. The toys were as neglected and faded as some of the kids she had seen. Some lawns seemed more like jungles with broken down cars jutting up from the tall weeds. Numbers were missing from many of the mailboxes, but Jessica was finally able to spot the house where she had seen Aaron's car before. His car was still there. She still couldn't get a feel for what kind of car it was. It was a faded green color and was shaped like a narrow Kleenex box. She parked in the street across from the house and sat a few moments still looking around and planning what she was going to try to say once she saw Aaron.

An older car sat in his driveway next to Aaron's car. It looked as though it had been in a wreck but never repaired. The whole passenger side was mangled. The back window had been broken out and in its place was a piece of plastic that closely resembled a black trash bag. The plastic had been duct-taped around the edges. She felt sorry for Aaron. This place was a mess. She shuddered at the thought of him living here. There was also a car with a brand new paint job parked diagonally across his yard. Jessica thought it must be the prized race car that Aaron and his father worked on together. She wasn't really "into" cars, but she knew a Ford Mustang when she saw one. This one had two white stripes down its hood. She thought it must be a specialty car with that paint job. It was by far the nicest car on the block.

Finally, she took a deep breath and forced herself to do what she came to do. She stepped out of her own car and made her way to the front porch. It was barely bigger than she was. Jessica looked around some more before knocking on the door. Dull red paint was chipping off the sides of the house. Jessica had always thought of wood as being lightly colored with a certain glossiness to it. The exposed wood she saw was dull and gray looking. The missing paint had been gone a long time.

Thinking about actually knocking on the door made Jessica's heart speed up to twice its normal pace. She started getting more nervous -- really nervous. What if someone angrily slammed the door in her face? What if Aaron wouldn't speak to her after all? What if she was totally wrong about the dreams?

Wrestling with her thoughts, Jessica finally decided she had to try. It was now or never. She knew it was around eight o'clock on a Saturday morning, but she just had to talk to Aaron. Her eyes blazed with determination as she raised her hand to knock on the door. Knock, Knock, Knock. She did it. Seconds went by and no one answered. She tried knocking again a little louder; still, no answer. Maybe they weren't home.

Jessica waited a few more seconds. She considered just leaving when suddenly she heard movements from the other side of the door. Someone unlocked a dead bolt. The she heard the sliding of a chain lock. The doorknob finally turned and the door creaked open. Standing in front of her was a woman whose skin was darker than her own. She had circles under her eyes and many creases in her face. Jessica thought the woman must have been very beautiful in her youth, but looked tired and worn down now. The woman had a head full of thick, beautiful dark brown hair. Jessica knew this had to be Aaron's mother.

The woman exclaimed in a hoarse voice, "We're not buying anything, and we don't need advice on your God."

Jessica, surprised by the reaction, quickly came to her own defense. "Oh, I am not selling anything, ma'am. I came to speak with Aar ... I mean A.J."

The woman without expression turned and yelled into the house, "A.J.! A.J.! You have someone here to see you."

'What am I doing?' Jessica thought to herself.

This was it. She was finally going to talk to Aaron about the dreams. She started twitching one foot and rubbing her hands. She hoped everything would go smoothly. She was so nervous she wanted to vomit.

Aaron came to the doorway; his eyes squinted in the morning sun. He was wearing old sweatpants that had a hole over one knee and no shirt. Jessica found her eyes exploring his bare chest. He looked so thin but muscular at the same time. He simply looked at Jessica and muttered, "Umm, hell... o?!"

Expecting a little more of a greeting than that, Jessica hesitated before responding, "Hi. I know this may be a little early. I'm sorry if I woke you up, but this is very, very important. Can we go somewhere to talk?"

Awkwardly, Aaron looked at her and said, "Yeah, what's this about?"

"I'd rather talk somewhere where no one is around. Just trust me on this. I promise it won't take long. I have doughnuts in the car," she said as she flashed a pleading smile at him.

Aaron turned back toward the inside of his house and yelled, "Mom, I'll be back in a little while," and closed the door. As soon as the door shut, he realized he didn't have shoes or a shirt on, so he smiled at Jessica and said, "Just a minute."

He went back inside and reappeared in a few moments with shoes and a t-shirt, but no socks. Silently he followed Jessica to her car and plopped down in the passenger seat. Jessica sat properly behind the wheel on the driver's side.

"This is a nice ride," he commented. "Is this an '83 or '84?"

"It's an '83," she answered. "So do you know a place around here where we can talk? You know, like a park or soccer fields or something?"

Aaron, looking a little more awake now said, "Yeah, you need to go up two blocks, and there will be an alley on the right. Turn down it. There is a little park that not very many people know about. So is this car yours or your parents?"

"It's mine," Jessica replied not knowing whether to be proud or feel guilty.

"Damn, you must have a lot of money then."

Jessica just kept her eyes on the road through an awkward silence. She smiled and changed the subject. After all it wasn't anything she had done. Her father was the one with all the money. Not her. "So help yourself to the doughnuts. I brought you chocolate milk as well."

"Nice. Thanks. Oh, turn right -- right here. It's kind of hard to see."

Jessica turned a sharp right. Luckily, Aaron hadn't opened his milk yet and the doughnuts were still packaged, or there might have been a mess as the bag slid off the seat and launched into the floorboard at Aaron's feet.

"Now, there'll be in opening in the houses, again to your right, behind this first house."

Sure enough, as Jessica pulled past the side of the first house there was a huge opening with a city park tucked inside. There were swings and play equipment for children. Jessica never would have guessed there was a park here. Around the remaining perimeter there were houses that were built side by side in a semi-circle. It resembled a cul-de-sac, only the houses faced away, and there wasn't a dead end street. The alley was the only way to get to the park. Jessica was captivated by its beauty. She looked around and spotted picnic tables as well. Jessica parked the car, got out, and stood in amazement.

Aaron stepped out of the car too, and interrupted her thoughts, "We call this Hidden Park. You can probably figure out why."

It took a few minutes, but Jessica started realizing she recognized some things. The way the swings and the park bench were positioned and the half empty sandbox next to the slide stirred warm, dream-like memories. She got goose bumps. This was the park in her dreams. "Aaron, I need to show you something, and I need you to tell me if you know anything about it."

Jessica nervously unbuttoned the top two buttons of her shirt. She then pinched the cross shaped pendant between her index finger and thumb and pulled it out for him to see. "Do you recognize this, Aaron?"

Aaron's face turned pale. He slowly looked at Jessica and then at the necklace. They both stood in silence.

Aaron put his hands on top of his head, closed his eyes, and exhaled loudly. "Wow, I...I don't know what to say."

Jessica again asked, "Do you recognize this? You have to be honest with me because, to be honest, I'm a little freaked out right now."

Aaron nodded, "Yes, I do. It is my grandmother's necklace."

"So how did I end up with it?" She knew he had given it to her in a dream, but wasn't ready to tell him that part yet.

Aaron, on the other hand, was more direct and got right to the point, "Do you dream very much?"

"Yes!"

Both stared at the other one in silence.

Jessica broke in and said, "I actually had a dream last night. Then I woke up this morning and was wearing this."

Aaron raised his eyebrows as he said, "Tell you what. Let's get the doughnuts and milk out of the car and sit down at the picnic table. Then I will tell you what I know, and you can tell me what you know."

They walked back to the car. Aaron grabbed the doughnuts from the floorboard while Jessica searched her car for napkins. They sat across from each other at the picnic table. Aaron started the conversation again, "Well, I have dreams, too. I hope it doesn't freak you out when I tell you what I dreamed last night." Dream by dream they shared what they remembered from each one. The results were shocking. They were sharing the same dreams.

"So how does this happen, and what does it all mean?" Jessica inquired.

"You want the long version or the short version?" Aaron asked.

Jessica answered, "Long. I want to know EVERYTHING you know so I can understand this."

Aaron began, "The long version it is. Well, my grandmother was the best grandma any kid could ever want. She used to read to me all the time and whenever she didn't have a book to share she would tell me stories. I remember I couldn't wait for Grandma to visit because she had a way of making the whole world so interesting. She traveled to many countries and experienced life to the fullest.

"I remember, just before she died, she started telling me of how each one of us has a soul mate somewhere in the world. She said Grandpa Jones was hers, and that she would be with him again someday -- because he died a year ago. I thought it was just another one of her stories. Grandpa Jones was her second husband. She called him her soul mate, and she always told me that I had a soul mate out there, too. She told me that when we are apart from our soul mate the universe opens up and gives us repeated opportunities to unite with this person. If the opportunities don't happen fast enough or if the people don't take the opportunities given, the souls will go out in the night while you sleep and search for each other themselves. It is during your dreams that the soul reveals to you who and where your soul mate is. She said she spent over half her life denying the opportunity to be with Grandpa Jones, but when they got together, she said it was the happiest day of her life. See, she had been married to Grandpa Howser for over 20 years before it ended in divorce. She said it was awful because they divorced in a time when it wasn't very common. A few years later, Grandpa Howser moved away and no one in the family heard from him again."

Aaron took a deep breath, and then continued, "Told you this was long." Jessica just smiled taking it all in.

"Then one day out of the blue she introduces us to the man who became Grandpa Jones. I was fine with him. He was nice, and he made my Grandma so happy. They started traveling together and, before we knew it, they were married. He was really nice to all of her grandkids. One Christmas he gave me a handmade box carved out of cedar. I used it to hold rocks and other odds and ends. He died of cancer suddenly the next year. Grandma was heartbroken. Her health started to deteriorate as well, and she had to be hospitalized. About a month before she died, she called me in to her hospital room alone. She told me she had something special she wanted me to keep. She had me go to the closet and get a little cloth bag out of her purse. It was that necklace."

Aaron pointed to it. "She told me to not underestimate the power of my soul. To let it guide me in life. She told me to take the necklace and keep it in the cedar box Grandpa Jones had made for me. She said when my soul finds its mate, it would find the necklace and take it to her. I was to do nothing but wait. She didn't want me to lose half a lifetime with the wrong girl. She said she didn't give it to my father because he never listened to his heart anyway and repeatedly ignored any advice she had ever given him. She said a lot of his unhappiness came from not being true to who he was supposed to be. I did what she asked out of respect, but, honestly, I never believed it would actually happen. I'm not sure how she got the necklace."

Jessica replied, "That is the most beautiful and amazing story I have ever heard."

Aaron stood up, scratched his head, and came around to sit right beside Jessica. He continued, "Thanks, but it just complicated my life tremendously. When I thought I was just dreaming, I could write it off as 'just a dream.' Now I can't." Staring off into the distance, they just sat and felt the comfort of being near each other in real life. Overpowered by the complexity of the situation, they were enjoying every second in the other one's presence.

Jessica broke in, "So what do you want to do? Do you want the necklace back? It is rightfully yours."

"No, you keep it. I have to honor my grandma's wishes. So, while we are talking about all this -- I know I'm changing the subject a little – but, in the dreams I see things that happen to you. Are those things true?"

Suddenly Jessica became uncomfortable. She didn't like the thought of his knowing everything about her. It was fine in the dreams, but it scared the hell out of her in real life. She side stepped it with her own question: "You first. I have seen some awful things happen to you, too. Are those real?"

"Yep," was Aaron's only response. He obviously wasn't ready to talk about that part of it either.

"Me, too," Jessica whispered.

The singing of birds in the distance was the only sound as Jessica and Aaron sat silently next to one another and let their thoughts spiral and whirl in their own minds.

Jessica broke the silence. "So, do think we should try being a part of each other's lives?"

Her question was met with an awkward silence as Aaron thought long and hard. He closed his eyes for several heartbeats before opening them with his decision.

"Jesse, I would love to sweep you off your feet and show you the world. I would love to take you away from your dad. I would love to live in a perfect world where our social status didn't matter, and we were free to be with whomever we wanted. But, I can't, for the life of me, see that happening right now. I think you are beautiful. I thought you were beautiful before I met you in person. You are everything I have always wished for, but it can't work. Not right now. We come from two different worlds. I just don't see how someone like you and someone like me can possibly make it work, at least not right now. Your friends wouldn't accept me any more than my friends would accept you."

Jessica's eyes started turning red as she was holding back the tears. She knew he had a point, but she didn't want it to be that way. It was frustrating. She was actually stunned by her own physical reaction. She stood up and looked the other way. She began desperately trying to think of a way to make it work. She had no answers either.

Aaron sadly watched her and could feel his heart sink as well. He walked up to her, put his hands on her shoulders and turned her around to look at him. He then put his arms around her and held her close to him. Jessica laid her head against his chest, comforted by the sound of his heart beating beneath her ear. She wrapped her arms around his body. For that one moment in time everything felt perfect. They lingered in the embrace.

"I want to figure something out -- even if it can't last," Jessica confessed.

Aaron took his hands and cupped Jessica's face. He gently tilted her head up so they could see each other eye to eye. "Okay."

Before either one of them realized what was going on, Aaron instinctively lowered his lips to hers. Just like the dreams, there was a spark between them that was undeniably a source to be reckoned with. They both felt it from the tips of their heads to the tips of their toes. They had to try to find a way to be near each other. They both knew it.

"Okay, we need time to think this through. How about for now we just develop our friendship with no strings attached. Then, when the timing is right, we can try seeing each other exclusively. I just think we need to take this slow," Aaron suggested.

"Agreed! It's the most complicated thing I have ever experienced, so I certainly would like to take it nice and slow." Jessica smiled then asked playfully, "So, do you like to swing?"

"I did when I was like five," Aaron answered somewhat sarcastically.

"Well, Mr. 'I'm too cool to swing,' I'll race ya over there," Jessica took off sprinting towards the nearest set of swings.

Aaron followed in hot pursuit. It was actually no contest. Jessica was fast, but Aaron was quite a bit faster.

He hit the swings first and yelled triumphantly, "I win!"

"Oh, shut up. I'm sure you cheated somehow," Jessica teased.

They both laughed and climbed onto their own swings. Time stood still as they enjoyed the park and each other. Reluctantly, Aaron finally brought them back to reality as he made a comment about getting home to finish some chores. They dismounted and headed toward the car.

Jessica said, "Aaron, I had a lot of fun with you. Can I ask you a favor though?"

"Anything," was his reply.

"The stuff we talked about today. Please don't tell anyone about my dad. I don't want anyone to find out. It could destroy our family. I will deal with it in my own way."

One side of Aaron's lip curled up in a smile. "You have my word. I'd like the same favor in return."

"You got it. It's our secret. Well, along with the dreams and everything else, too."

They smiled conspiratorially at each other.

As they entered the car Aaron reminded Jessica of another so-called-problem. "Jesse, I need our time together to be kept a secret for now as well. I need to work things out with Ronda. She would kill both of us if she knew about this morning."

"My lips are ABSOLUTELY sealed on that one!" Jessica agreed wholeheartedly.

Bringing up Ronda's name made Jessica a little jealous and a little worried. She was so happy to have shared this time with Aaron. She was excited to think that one day they might be together, but she was also a bit sad that it might take a long time before they could figure out how they could make it work.

Jessica stopped the car in front of Aaron's house. "Wait, Aaron. I have an idea. Why don't I give the necklace back to you as a test? If I get it back, we know your grandma was right for sure. If I don't then maybe this is just some weird, unexplainable mistake.

Aaron thought for a moment, "Okay, let's do that. Come in with me a second."

They both stepped out of the car and Aaron led her to the front door. He quietly turned the knob. As he did, he looked back to Jessica and put his index finger to his lips as if to say, "Shhhhh." The two tip-toed through the doorway into the house. Aaron whispered, "Follow me."

The only light in the house came from the windows. Jessica didn't want to be nosey so she tried not to look around. She simply followed Aaron down a bare hallway. He opened another door leading into his bedroom. There wasn't much furniture at all in his room. His bed, stuck in the corner, consisted only of a mattress directly on the floor with sheets lying in disarray on top. In another corner stood a single dresser with what looked like clean clothes folded and stacked on top. Aaron's closet had a brown imitation wood door on it. He opened it. Jessica looked in his closet and found that it held only about ten shirts and a couple of pairs of jeans. There were two shelves at the top on which sat the cedar box he'd mentioned. Aaron took hold of the box with one hand and pulled it down close to him. He opened the lid; there were a few little rocks and pop tops in it.

Jessica reached back to unhook the necklace but had trouble getting it off. Aaron set the box on top of his dresser and turned to help. Jessica held her hair off her neck while Aaron gently unhooked the necklace. She caught it in her hands as the chains fell apart. She placed it in the cedar box. "It's ready for the big test," Aaron said as he secured the lid to the top and placed it back on the shelf.

Jessica was nervous. She could never predict when she would have a dream, so she had no idea how long it would be until she had another one. What if she didn't have any more? What if this was just a one-time thing? It was time to just sit tight, and that made Jessica uneasy.

Aaron walked her back to the front door. The moment she reached her car, she looked back. Aaron was leaning up against the door frame. She waved, and he waved back. This was it; this was the test to see if they were supposed to be together or not. If so, they would just have to figure out what was next.

As she drove away she uttered to herself, "Soul mates, I like that."

Chapter 7

The Meetings

Going to school and sitting in the same classroom with Aaron without being able to openly show their friendship was extremely hard for Jessica, and it was getting harder each passing day. She figured it had to be getting harder for Aaron as well. He was so close, yet he was so far. Occasionally, their eyes met, and Aaron's lips would roll up into a smile that would melt Jessica's heart. He was so incredibly handsome. His piercing blue eyes made Jessica want to lose herself in them. There were also times they would pass each other in the hall and have to pretend not to know one another. Not yet. The absolute worst time for Jessica was when she saw Aaron at lunch sitting next to Ronda. Ronda would be hanging all over Aaron, and it made Jessica sick to her stomach with jealously. She also began to wonder why it was taking Aaron so long to get rid of Ronda and why she hadn't had another dream yet.

Why was he bothering with Ronda if he believed his grandma? Wasn't she his soul mate? Time would tell. Jessica also began to notice the longer Aaron was at the high school, the more girls seemed to like him. A lot of girls had crushes on him now. As far as Jessica knew, none of her closest friends did, but he was the type of guy those girls would crush on in secret. They wouldn't claim it to anyone. He wasn't an athlete and he certainly wasn't rich. He didn't meet their standards. He was a bad boy -- a really, really cute bad boy.

Finally, one night she entered a dream after a long night of studying.

The sun was shining down on Jessica as she sat in a swing at Hidden Park. As always the birds were singing and a cool breeze tickled the back of her neck. Aaron approached from the alley entrance. Jessica lit up with a smile and ran to him. He picked her up off the ground like a child and swung her around in a circle. As he sat her back on the ground the two embraced in a kiss. This time there were no bad memories to see. It was just the two of them on a beautiful day.

Once their lips parted, Jessica stared into Aaron's eyes and said, "You made it! You finally made it! I was beginning to worry!"

"I had to see you. Of course, I came!" Aaron kissed her once more.

"I believe you left something at my house, "he whispered in her ear as he secured the necklace around her neck.

Jessica giggled, "I love this necklace. Thank you, Aaron."

The two sat down at the picnic table and talked about how school was going and how they longed to be together. As they talked, a spider scurried across the table. Jessica jumped to her feet to get away from it. Aaron looked at her and said, "Don't be afraid. That's a sign. The spider represents infinite possibilities. It is a message to us to look beyond the web of confusion; the answer for our situation is out there."

Jessica sat back down and calmly watched as the spider jumped from the table to the ground. It was quite an amazing feat for something so small. "Where did you learn that?"

"Let's just say Grandma -- again. She taught me a lot about so many different things in life. She was part Cherokee Indian and wanted me to appreciate everything. I guess that makes me part Cherokee Indian as well. She said we are all tied together in this universe."

Jessica had never realized he was part Native American. She knew his skin appeared tan all the time, but she didn't put two and two together. It was never an issue. She was simply mesmerized by his knowledge.

"I think that's pretty cool," Jessica conceded, and she hugged him once more. She felt that all-too-familiar tugging to leave the dream. "I have to go now, but I look forward to seeing you again," she said in his ear. He kissed her cheek. She turned toward his lips and kissed him back.

"Good-bye, my soul mate!" was the last thing she said as she left.

Jessica awoke the next morning and felt the cross that hung around her neck. She smiled, and then she remembered the spider. They had to find a way to be together.

Three weeks passed after the encounter in the park. Jessica still continued to dream the most wonderful things about Aaron. It made her happy inside to know he was dreaming them also. They were so much alike in the dreams. They had so much fun together. In one dream he made her laugh so hard tears rolled down her cheeks. She loved his sense of humor. In another dream, her favorite, she had grabbed the baseball cap he was wearing and took off running through a field of tall grass and wildflowers. He chased after her saying she had better give the hat back "or else." Half way across the field he caught her from behind. Their laughter was swallowed by the miles of open country. Aaron threw his arm out snagging Jessica around the waist. Thrown off balance, both went tumbling to the ground. Breathless from the chase, they sat motionless gasping for fresh air.

Finally Aaron had looked at Jessica and said, "I told you not to steal my hat!"

Jessica had playfully challenged him by asking, "What are you going to do to stop me?"

In a split second Aaron had her pinned to the ground like a big brother wrestles a little brother into submission. He had each of her wrists held tightly in his hands and held them firm against the flattened grass.

Jessica remembered that in her dream she squealed, "That is so not fair! You are stronger than I am!"

Their eyes had locked in a stare. The chemistry between them had silenced everything. Aaron slowly lowered his head so his lips could capture hers. He kissed her with a yearning passion that made her feel alive. Jessica had never been kissed the way Aaron kissed her in that dream. Even when she awoke from the dream, his kisses would always linger on her lips and in her mind.

At school the next day, Aaron deliberately turned around in his chair first hour and winked at her. When he did, she softly bit her lower lip and smiled back. She knew it wouldn't be long before they would lose the ability hide their feelings for one another.

Day after day, week after week, dream after dream, Jessica's thoughts were more and more focused on Aaron. She got to the point that she decided she no longer was willing to wait for him to "settle things" with Ronda. She decided she was going to give him a deadline. She couldn't take this anymore.

There were so many qualities Aaron had that she admired and needed, yet there were still some things she didn't like. She didn't like the group he hung out with and the rumors about them. People said they were drinkers and partiers and often came to school with hangovers. She never addressed that with Aaron. She also suspected him of smoking. She knew everyone had their bad habits, but she really didn't like that one. Regardless of his image at school, their dreams were far more powerful, and she loved everything in them. She could openly talk to Aaron -- really talk to him in the dreams. He cared about what was going on in her life. She was falling in love with him. He was becoming her addiction. She needed him in order to get through each day. She needed him in order to get through the beatings at home. She needed him -- period.

Jessica had a plan to see Aaron, but it would take a little help from Suzie to pull it off. Suzie was an office aid. Jessica cornered her to find out when and if she would do her a favor.

"Of course," Suzie agreed.

"Could you possibly get me out of class with a fake note today? Last hour I'm just in art class. We never do much in there. I'm in Mr. Gregory's class."

Suzie's eyebrows shot up while she questioned, "Did I just hear you correctly, Ms. 'Play-by-the rules' Taylor ?"

Jessica, realizing Suzie couldn't believe what she was asking, tried to explain. "Look, I desperately need to talk to someone. It is really important to me, and I need your help. Will you please do it, just this once? I promise I will never ask you to do this again."

Suzie hugged Jessica suddenly. She looked at Jessica's confused face and laughed.

"Welcome to the dark side. I've been waiting for this day, my friend, when you would become a real teenager!" Suzie teased Jessica.

Jessica looked around nervously, as if she didn't quite know how to take Suzie.

Suzie decided to try again, a little more seriously. "Sure, if it is really that important to you. It's not a big deal at all. We office aids have a system we perfected for this kind of thing. You're not the first to ask, ya know. What time do you need out of class?"

"How about right after class starts? Can you get this other person out, too?"

"Only if you tell me who this other person is." Suzie reminded Jessica that she was not a mind reader.

Taking a deep breath she quickly whispered, "A.J. Howser."

"Jessica," Suzie said half laugh laughing, "Ummm, do you remember the incident in the bathroom several months ago? That's crazy. Or is there something you are not telling me about that I should know?"

Understanding Suzie's shock, Jessica calmly explained to her that she had a class with him, and she just needed to talk with him. She figured that if she did it this way, it would be in secret, and Ronda wouldn't find out. Plus, his classmates would just assume he was in trouble and not question it. Jessica felt it was the perfect plan. After a few seconds, Suzie nodded her head. The plan was in place. If Jessica's plan worked, no one would ever guess they were together. 'No one' in Jessica's mind meant Ronda.

"Okay, girl, I will do it for you. I don't really believe you are thinking clearly, but it's your call. Also, when it's all said and done you **have** to share the details with me! I know there is something going on that you haven't been telling me!" Suzie blackmailed the truth from her friend.

"Deal!" Jessica said through her smile as she walked on to her next class.

The bell for the last hour classes rang. Jessica was in her seat as the teacher was instructing students to get out their sketch pads. Jessica stared at the door. She seemed to feel every second that ticked by. Finally, after three agonizing minutes of class, Suzie pranced in with a white slip of paper stating: "Jessica Taylor had to go to the office *immediately*." The teacher handed her the note and continued talking about the lesson. Suzie left the classroom with Jessica several steps behind.

Once in the hall, Suzie swung around and

reminded Jessica, "Call me after school and tell me EVERYTHING! Okay?"

"I will. Now which room is Aaron coming out of?"

"Oh, he is in room 234 on the second floor. Clint left to take the note to him the same time I left to get you. Of course, you are much closer, but he'll be headed this way in no time."

Knowing which room he was coming from helped Jessica determine her route to intercept him before he actually reached the office. That would be horrible if she missed him, and he actually did go into the office to see the principal. Then the principal would realize the office aids were passing fake notes to get friends out of class. It really did happen a lot. All the kids knew it anyway. Just no grown-ups were suspicious yet, thank goodness. At least, she didn't think they were.

Jessica trotted softly down the hall. She did slow to a walk as she passed a classroom door that was open. Clint passed her going the opposite direction. He had several white little notes in his hands. They smiled at each other. She knew Aaron had to be only steps behind. She was right. He rounded the corner and started heading her way. A look of surprise covered his face as he made eye contact with Jessica.

She walked right up to him and mumbled, "That was a fake note. I had it sent to you. Follow me."

They retraced his path back to the stairway he had just used to come down to the first floor. He followed several feet behind, so it looked like a coincidence that they were in the hall at the same time. Once at the stairway, instead of ascending, they actually went down another flight to the basement. It was creepy and dark in that stairwell, and students didn't normally go down there -- unless he or she had been dared.

Jessica led him down a dark hallway to a wooden door. It had a sign attached to it that read: *Cheer Closet - Keep Out.* Quietly she reached in her pants pocket and pulled out a shiny silver key, and she opened the lock that kept intruders out. They stepped inside to total blackness. Jessica raised her hand in the air searching for the familiar string that hung down from the sole light fixture. She tugged on it and instantly the room was flooded with light. Jessica took a step back over to the door and closed it. There was another lock on the inside that slid across securing the door shut.

"If you couldn't tell, this is the cheerleading storage room," she said as Aaron looked around.

He saw boxes and boxes of old pom-pons, posters that read, "Go, Fighting Irish," shelves full of miscellaneous gadgets, paint cans, paint brushes, and a megaphone.

"Hmmmm, couldn't tell," he replied sarcastically. "So is this kidnapping?" Aaron wiggled his eyebrows at Jessica.

"Ha-ha, very funny. I just wanted to talk, and we never get a chance to. I figured this would be a way we could actually see each other without anyone knowing about it. So what do you think?" Jessica questioned.

"Wow, I'm impressed. Well, as long as we don't get caught, that is. So how did you manage this 007?" Aaron jokingly inquired.

Jessica explained how she executed her plan and why she chose the cheer closet. No one ever seemed to go into the basement. It was just used as storage. The janitor would be down there at certain times of the day, but for the most part it was vacated. Jessica had seen the janitor mopping the cafeteria so she knew it would be empty.

"So what made you want to do this?" Aaron asked.

Jessica took a deep cleansing breath. She looked at Aaron, and felt her heart beating faster. He always made her feel dizzy, and her heart seemed to skip a beat.

"Well, I really wanted to talk to you in person. It has been a while since we talked at Hidden Park. It was my understanding from that meeting that we would try to slowly work on a friendship, and you were going to square things away with Ronda. Did I get that wrong? Because we still don't talk, and as far as I can see, everything else is the same." She paused and waited for Aaron's response.

"Yeah, I know. I just haven't figured out what to do without it looking really strange. I would love to be with you somehow, but you know as well as I do that we live in different worlds. We always have. I can't change that just because I want to," Aaron started.

Jessica interrupted, "Well, I'm not ready to just give up yet. We are still having our dreams. I have the necklace again. We are meant to be together regardless of what others think. I have thought about this a lot. Ever since you told me the story about your grandma and how our souls are searching for each other, I really think we owe it to ourselves to try and make it work. We have a wonderful time in the dreams. Then, when I come to school – well -- it's like you don't even know me. Sometimes I just wish we could go to lunch together or walk down the hall. I wish we could have a conversation in our first hour class -- something! I would settle for anything, Aaron, except being ignored," Jessica released her pent up frustrations.

"Jesse, I'm so sorry. I know how you feel, and you have to trust me when I say that I want the same things. I honestly do! I'm just really confused. Jesse, think about it. Look at who you are and who I am. Haven't you realized yet that … that … I'm not good enough for you?! You need someone better than me," Aaron finally admitted his fears, "regardless of the necklace."

"You're wrong. It's in the dreams, Aaron. Think about our dreams. No matter what goes on, we are supposed to be together. I don't want anyone else. I want to be with you," Jessica surprised herself with her own words. She usually wasn't this direct, especially when talking to guys.

"Don't take this wrong, Jesse, but think about it this way. Would you go out between classes and smoke with me? Would you go to keg parties and get wasted with me on the weekends? Would you want to ride motorcycles with me? What would we possibly do together? There is more to a relationship then just dreaming about the other one. Jesse, trust me. I'm not the kind of guy you need. Your friends know that. Just think of how Suzie would respond if she saw you with me. She gives me nonstop dirty looks already! She wouldn't tolerate your being with me. You don't see that side of me in the dreams, but that is who I am in real life," Aaron leveled with her.

His words silenced her for a moment. He did have a point. It bothered her to think that he did all those things. She never associated with people who were like that. Suzie, on the other hand, might be more understanding than he gave her credit for. Jessica grew a little angry. It wasn't fair!

"That is the part *you* don't get. You think that I care about what others think of me, and I don't. No, I don't smoke, and, no, I wouldn't get wasted, but we could find other things to do. So is that why you are still with Ronda even though you told me you were going to … let's see … how'd you say it? Oh, yeah, 'work things out' with her? Is she that kind of girl?" Jessica blurted out.

"She has nothing to do with this. I am still with her because I can't seem to break it off. We have a lot in common. Even if I don't dream about her, she is a good friend, and I don't have to worry about her judging me for who I'm not and what I don't have." Aaron snapped.

Jessica looked away. She felt a swirl of anger, frustration, jealousy, betrayal, and sadness.

"So do you like her better than me?" she asked.

Aaron slowly shook his head, "That's not fair."

"Not fair? Well, I'll tell you what's not fair; the fact that I have finally found someone who is supposed to be my soul mate, and he is off dating another girl. The fact that he knows my deepest darkest secret, things I wish NO ONE knew ever!!

Then tells me he cares about me, but acts as though I don't exist in public. That's what is not fair!" The words tumbled angrily from Jessica's lips.

Frustrated as well, Aaron confessed, "I agree, it is not fair. Jesse, I care about you so much. I have been up-front about that all along. This situation is weird for me. I honestly don't know what I am supposed to do. I feel trapped between two worlds. One is ideal and one is real. We live in the *real* world that is not perfect. I don't know what else I can say."

"Maybe it's *you* who cares too much about what others think," Jessica was now close to tears.

She had hoped that this secret meeting would turn out well, but it hadn't so far. A silence fell over them both.

Aaron finally broke the silence by saying, "I don't want to hurt you, Jesse. If we were together, I am afraid you would be disappointed. No, I *know* you would be disappointed."

"Mmm" was her only audible response, not giving Aaron any clue about what was going through her mind.

He continued, "I am afraid if you really, really knew me, you wouldn't like who I am. I have tried to tell you this a million times, and you just won't listen. I just don't think you truly would want to be with someone like me. You don't know what you are getting into. I am different in those dreams than I am here."

She looked Aaron in the eye. He could see the hurt and frustration reflected in her eyes that were welling with tears.

"Why can't I decide for myself? I know that

you are a good person inside and nothing will change my opinion of that. Why are you so afraid?"

Out of nowhere an idea hit her.

"Why not meet me on the weekends at Hidden Park? Just give me time to get to know you in the real world." She wondered why she hadn't thought of that sooner. Of course, meeting at their park would be perfect!

Aaron looked dumbfounded. It obviously hadn't crossed his mind before either. He was looking for a reason that it wouldn't work, but he thought of nothing. He knew better than anyone that not very many people ever used the park.

He smiled, "All right -- I'll do that. Are you sure?"

"Yes, let's meet at 8:00 again Saturday morning. That way I can get out before my parents wake up, and they won't be asking me a lot of questions."

Aaron was not thrilled at all about the early morning, but he was willing to try it for now. He really did want to be with Jessica, he was just scared.

"Saturday morning at 8:00. Hidden Park. I will be there," he confirmed.

"Great!" Jessica squealed.

She was so excited she flung her arms around him and gave him a big hug. Then she realized he may not want to be hugged and dropped her arms quickly. She apologized.

Quickly Aaron responded, "Please, don't apologize. And ... you didn't have to let go."

They smiled at each other and embraced in

another hug. It felt so good to be able to touch in person. It felt just like it did in the dreams -- perfect. Jessica had never noticed it in the dreams, but now being so close to him, her cheek pressed against his chest, she noticed she could smell him. She couldn't put her finger on it, but he smelled so good. She closed her eyes and inhaled. She wanted the embrace to last forever. She felt safe in his arms.

After a moment, Aaron looked down to make eye contact with Jessica. Just like in the dreams, he couldn't seem to stop himself from kissing her. She did nothing to stop him either. The electricity surged through her body. Even though he had a girlfriend, for this moment in time Jessica pretended he was all hers. She didn't care about the consequences if Ronda found out. Aaron was hers. She knew it, Aaron knew it, and the universe had to know it as well. Everything about it felt so right, even if she had to fight to keep it.

No one found out about the meeting in the basement. When Jessica called Suzie that evening she told her that she really did have a crush on him. She begged Suzie to not tell anyone because of the Ronda situation. Suzie agreed, mainly because she didn't want Ronda to come after her either. Suzie was supportive of Jessica because she was her closest friend, but still not clear on why she liked someone like A.J. Suzie wanted to know if they were going to start seeing each other. Jessica told her she didn't think so; they were just going to have a secret friendship. That's all.

Saturday morning couldn't arrive soon enough. Aaron rode his bike, and Jessica drove her car. Both had a wonderful time talking about what they had dreamed of during the week, as well as what had been going on in their lives at school. They talked a little about their lives away from school, too. Neither knew what would become of their relationship, but both felt they had to try to get to know each other in real life. Their meetings were secret to the rest of the world, just like the dreams, just like their abusive home lives, just like this park -- all one big secret. They were the only two who knew the truth, and this secret solidified their bond.

They played a game taking turns asking each other questions about their likes and dislikes. They took breaks to swing or play in dirt. Aaron knew a lot about birds, animals, and insects (which no one at school would ever know about him). He taught Jessica how to identify them and educated her on their behaviors. The most fascinating one to her was the one he called a doodle bug. She couldn't see the bug, but it had little traps in the dirt. It hid underground below the trap so if an ant happened to walk over it, the dirt would swallow it up like quicksand and the bug ate it.

It amazed Jessica how smart he really was and how no one at the school would ever guess how complex his thinking process could be. Why he hid his intelligence and why he wanted others to see him as a bad boy were mysteries to her. He had a cold exterior but a gentle caring interior. Their Saturday morning together was all she had hoped it to be. Everything just felt so right.

The Saturday meeting made sitting through school the next week a little easier on Jessica. At least, when they made eye contact they could smile. Even in the hallway where everyone could see, they would smile. When they passed each other they would either smile or show a small wave. The only time that wasn't the case was when Ronda was near Aaron. If she saw Ronda anywhere around, Jessica would go the other way so it was not possible to make eye contact. This went on for weeks. Jessica didn't like that at all. She could not figure out for the life of her why Aaron hadn't broken it off with Ronda.

Another Saturday morning rolled around. Jessica woke up before her alarm. The meeting with Aaron was to be at 8:00, as always. She bounced out of bed early, ate breakfast, showered and was ready to leave by 7:30. She arrived 15 minutes early. It didn't matter; she would just sit at the picnic table and listen to the birds. She never realized how their singing relaxed her. The morning air was a little brisk but so refreshing. She loved mornings.

Eight o'clock came and went. There was no sign of Aaron. Jessica worried because he had always been on time before. All she could do was wait for him. Aaron finally showed up about 8:20. His hair was matted on the top of his head, his eyes were bloodshot, his clothing extremely wrinkled.

"Good morning, sleeping beauty!" Jessica welcomed him.

He mumbled, "Yeah, morning."

Jessica watched him as he clumsily approached the picnic table where she sat.

"What's wrong, Aaron? Are you sick?" Jessica asked, worried.

Avoiding eye contact he replied, "One might call it that."

Jessica suspiciously looked him over head to toe. "Something isn't right. You're acting weird. What's the matter?"

"I'm here, what does it matter?" Aaron replied defensively.

"I'm just worried, that's all," she said.

"I told you," Aaron dismissed her concerns.

"You told me what?" Jessica asked, not really following his logic.

"I told you I would disappoint you," Aaron stated matter-of-factly.

"I'm not following you, Aaron," Jessica admitted.

"I have a hangover, and I feel like shit, okay?" Aaron spat out sarcastically.

Jessica couldn't believe her ears. Well, she could, but she didn't want to. She knew he drank, and he even told her he got 'wasted' sometimes, but why did he have to do it right before their meeting? Actually, why did he have to do it ever? Didn't he understand that drinking for the sake of 'fun' was actually a self-destructive behavior? She learned about those in her psychology class. Anything that tears the body down – especially when the person does it with full knowledge that's it's unhealthy -- is a self-destructive act. It's as though the drinker is punishing himself or herself. Her thoughts were racing a mile a minute. She wanted to be rational and talk to Aaron calmly. She wanted not to make a big deal of this, but why, why, why did he feel the need to do this to himself?

With all these thoughts consuming her mind,

the only response she could muster was, "Oh."

She looked away.

Aaron simply laid his head down on his folded arms. For the first time, Jessica finally understood why Aaron was hesitant about a relationship with her. He was right about one thing; he had disappointed her. She tried to get a grip on this new anger bubbling up inside her. She didn't want to be angry at him. After all, she was the one who pushed the issue of being together in real life. She didn't know if she could stand being around another drinker. Her father was a drinker, and she hated him for the way he acted when he was drunk. Did Aaron become a different person when he was drunk? What if they had kids together one day, and what if one of those kids was a daughter? What if Aaron got drunk on a regular basis? How would he treat his own daughter? This thought was almost too much. She couldn't live with herself if …

"So are you mad at me, Jesse?" Aaron interrupted her thoughts from spiraling out of control and brought her back to the present.

She finally spoke up, "I don't know what I feel, to be honest."

She didn't want to say anything while her emotions were running high. She didn't want to say something then live to regret it.

They sat in silence a few more minutes. Jessica finally spoke up, "Do you understand why this is so upsetting for me?"

Aaron tried to look at her. His head was pounding, but he wanted to show her he respected her. "I could probably guess why."

"You are the only one who *would* be able to

understand me. When my father is sober, he is a very caring man. He tries to do what's right by my mother and me. But when he fills himself with ... whatever it is he drinks ... he becomes a monster. He is violent, and he becomes disgusting. The alcohol controls him and changes him. The saddest part is I don't think he remembers who he was when he was drunk. I don't think he remembers what he did to me. Do you know how bad I hate that? That is why I stay away from drinkers. It's not that I think I'm better than they are. I don't want to end up with someone who becomes a monster when he drinks. I don't want to be afraid to have children someday. Aaron, have you even really thought about what will happen to you as an adult? Look at how alcohol changes your dad. Did you know children of alcoholics have a greater chance of becoming alcoholics themselves? Your recreational drinking today could lead to becoming an alcoholic tomorrow."

Aaron was a little stunned. He guessed it might upset her, but he didn't think she would take it this hard.

"What if I told you I remember everything, and I do try to monitor how much I drink?" he inquired.

"I just question why you feel you need to do it at all? It is so unnecessary. There are so many things in life to give you a natural 'high.' Why do you have to do something that is so destructive?" Jessica argued.

Aaron blinked a few times then answered, "I guess, I like it. It helps me not think of all the shit that goes on in life. When I'm drunk, I don't have a care in the world. My father could hit me all he wanted to when I'm drunk, and I wouldn't feel it. It is my escape from everything ... life, my dad, Ronda bitchin' at me for stupid shit, now you bitchin' at me for being hung over. Plus, at the parties I'd look like an idiot if all my friends had beer, and I had a glass of milk."

Jessica broke in, "Aren't you the least bit scared about ending up like your father? Aren't you afraid of beating your own kids someday? You are going down the path he chose."

"Wait a second; I am nothing like my father! He is a jerk and always has been a jerk. I will not end up like him. I know when to stop. He doesn't!" Aaron defended himself.

"Aaron, there is no guarantee that you won't become an abusive alcoholic unless you make a conscious effort NOT to be like him," Jessica reasoned.

"You know, you aren't like this in the dreams," Aaron shot back.

That was the wrong thing to say. Like throwing gasoline onto a flame, Jessica became even more enraged. She felt as if she had been holding back a little, but now she was going to speak her mind.

"Well, you don't have a hangover in the dreams either. I promised myself I would never allow myself to fall for someone who drank. All my life I have had a plan because I am determined not to repeat the vicious cycle I'm caught in now. I try my hardest at everything I do. I make the best grades I can. I stay out of trouble. I take care of my body, and I play the game of life by the rules. I do this so I can get out of this place when I am eighteen. I am going to get away from this hell hole and make sure I put myself in the best position for opportunity. I am going to be successful and free. I am tired of waiting for happiness to find me. I am going to find my 'happily ever after' even if I have to fight hard to get it. I'm not going to let anyone ruin that for me. I don't want to bring kids into this world until I have figured out how to have a normal and happy family." Jessica let the words fall from her mouth in cascading waves of honesty.

"You make it sound like I don't want to be happy," replied Aaron.

Jessica continued more determined than ever, "You can't find happiness in a bottle, a package of cigarettes or a bong."

"Since you seem to be so hell-bent on finding your own happiness, tell me this, Jesse, why haven't you reported your dad for molesting and beating you? Why are you waiting until you're eighteen to just run away from all your problems? Why haven't you stopped them yourself? You want to judge me for dealing with my problems my way when you can't even take care of your own problems!" Aaron fired the questions at her in a stern voice.

His comments cut through her painfully, slicing her right down the middle of her chest and exposing everything that had been working to keep her alive. Now the question would be, could she stop the bleeding?

Jessica ran to her car, tears streaming down her face. How could he?

As she opened her car door she yelled back, "Fine, if that's the way you want play. You live your life, and I'll live mine. Just leave me alone. I don't **ever** want to talk to you again!"

Once home, Jessica went straight to her room. Her parents were still not up yet so her arrival went undetected. In her room she walked over to her jewelry box. She lifted the lid and music began to play. Her father had given it to her when he was on a business trip in Japan. It was hand crafted and absolutely beautiful.

Jessica listened to the music while she reached back to find the clasp to the cross necklace she had been wearing. This would be the first time since it was given back to her that she had taken it off. Until now, it had given her warm feelings every time she looked at it. It had served as a reminder that Aaron would always be close to her heart. Now, she no longer had the desire to wear it. She and Aaron were truly two different people living two different lives. How dare he think she could make all her problems go away so easily? It was so much more complicated than that. His comments made her feel as though he thought she brought the abuse on herself by not reporting it.

She removed the necklace and placed it in the jewelry box. Before closing the lid, she picked it up one last time and brought it to her lips. Something caught her eye. The tiny little ball on the inside of the cross that held the hearts seemed to have changed color. This morning when she left, each ball had a slightly pale blue tint to it -- the same blue hue they had when he first gave her the necklace. Now they looked a dark grey. She wasn't sure about her memory of it. Maybe she was remembering wrong. Who knew?

She also may have been wrong about trying

to meet with Aaron in person. Maybe he was right when he told her it would never work.   It was time to let go of the fantasy she had been living, believing she and Aaron were meant for each other. They were too different. She gently kissed the cross. A tear danced its way down her cheek onto her top lip and onto the necklace. She simply tucked the cross necklace away in the box and closed the lid. It was over. She had to move on.

Chapter 8

The Nightmare

It was the same old routine at school. Jessica had cheer practice, went to school, came home and did homework. After her several months of infatuation with Aaron, she needed to buckle down more on her grades. They had slipped a little so she had to work even harder to get them back up. Every chance there was extra credit assignment, Jessica did it. She studied her anatomy notes whether there was a test or not. She kept her personal calendar with her at all times, and wrote down every assignment that was given. She offered to write extra papers, to complete extra research, and do anything she could to get all her grades back up to high "A's."

Mrs. Willingham commented to her one day, "It's nice to have you back to your old ways, Ms. Taylor."

Things seemed back to normal. Even when Aaron came to class, they barely made eye contact. They had only had one dream since the argument. In the dream each apologized to the other and reminded each other of how much they were in love. Now, it just made Jessica mad to think about it. There seemed to be no parallel between the dreams and what was going on in real life. In her first dream she remembered his saying he was there to help her. Ha! What a joke. He was just there to complicate her life.

Midweek Suzie came rushing up to her,

"Jessica! I have great news. Mark asked me out!"

"Oh, I am so happy for you! You have liked him for a long time. Congratulations! So where are you two going?" Jessica asked automatically, only half way listening.

"Well, I'm not finished yet. He has a cousin who will be in town *this weekend.* He asked if I would find someone so we can double date. What do you say, Jessica? Doesn't that sound like fun?!" Suzie gushed enthusiastically.

Jessica's eyes widened, "For you! I have no idea what his cousin is like. You could be setting me up with a total creep. I don't know. Will you find out more about his cousin before I have to make a decision?"

"That's the best part. His cousin is a golfer at OU! He's a college guy! I don't know what he looks like but Mark says he is really cool. Come on Jessica, you have to go with me," Suzie begged.

Remembering she did owe her a favor, Jessica agreed. Both girls went giggling down the hall. It was such a relief to Jessica to actually be thinking about something other than her drama with Aaron.

Friday night rolled around quickly. The night before, Jessica and Suzie visited the mall to select the perfect outfits for their big double date. They met at Suzie's to get ready. Suzie had a huge full length mirror standing in one corner of her room, and another full length mirror that hung on the back of her door. It was set up to be able to see how you looked from all directions. Thankfully, it worked. They spent two full hours doing their hair, make-up and wardrobe.

Mark and his cousin, Steven, showed up at Suzie's house around 7:00 p.m. Suzie had noticed Mark earlier in the year when they had a class together. He was a baseball player. He was tall with dark blonde hair that had been bleached at the tips. All the baseball players did that to their hair to show team unity. His face was a deep bronze color from so many hours of practicing and playing outside, and he had eyes the color of milk chocolate. Plus, he had a muscular build. His arms and chest were very developed for a high school boy. Jessica thought he and Suzie looked really cute together.

Suzie was Jessica's exact opposite. Jessica had blue eyes, Suzie had brown. Jessica had blonde hair, Suzie had dark brown hair. Jessica had a fair complexion and Suzie tanned easily. Jessica thought Suzie was beautiful and deserved a guy like Mark.

Her first impression of her own date, Steven, was a good one. He stood about two inches taller than Mark and looked very athletic as well. He was just a leaner version of Mark. His hair was darker than his cousin's, but they had the same big brown eyes. Jessica was pleased with her first blind date. After introductions, the four of them were off to a dinner reservation at the *Steak de Maison*. Mark drove with Suzie in the passenger seat while Steven and Jessica were in the back.

Conversation was easy with Steven. He was three years older than Jessica and she loved his sense of humor. He had traveled extensively with his parents, and then traveled with his college golf team all over the country. He was an honor roll student, and had never had a serious girlfriend. He seemed so interesting compared to all the guys in her high school.

Jessica shared with him about herself as well. She opened up and told him about all the traveling she had done with her parents. She never really had talked about that with other people because she always felt like she was bragging. It didn't feel that way with Steven because he had been to more places than she had. They both had flown to other countries; they both had been on a cruise; they both had been to over half of the United States. It was nice talking to someone on the same level.

Dinner was fabulous. The house specialty was the steak. It was easily the best steak in that area. All four of them filled themselves with the delicious food and good company. The evening couldn't have been scripted any better. After the meal, they caught a movie. The movie ended around 11:00 p.m. and Jessica's curfew was midnight. When they exited the theatre, Mark noticed how clear the sky was and wanted to take Steven to a cool dock where you could see the stars better. They hopped in the car and drove to the nearest public lake that was on the outskirts of town.

Jessica reminded Mark she had to be home by midnight. He told her it would be no problem. They had almost an hour, and they were just going to this one dock that was fairly close. The winding road they were on ended at the lake. The further they got away from the center of town where all the lights were, the brighter the stars seemed.

Mark parked the car. Suzie, Jessica and Steven climbed out to take in the view. Mark motioned for them to follow him. He took them on a walking trail that lead to a small dock. The two couples talked and teased each other as they walked along the darkened trail. They emerged from the trail, walked out on the dock, and looked around.

The sight was truly amazing. Moonlight glittered off the tiny lake waves like a shimmering sea of diamonds. The lake was surrounded by the dark outlines of tall oak trees. Lonely crickets sang out to find one another. No one was around. No motors to drown out the sounds of the lake lapping at the shore or the occasional splash of a fish jumping out of the water to nab a bug on the surface. No human voices in the background like in town -- just a quiet calm.

Mark said, "Here is what my dad and brother like to do."

He sat down on the wooden dock and stretched his legs out in front of him. He leaned back until he was lying flat.

"Look at the stars this way guys," Mark suggested.

Everyone followed his lead and lay down on the dock. No one spoke for several minutes. The stars seemed to have multiplied. They could see so many more out here than they ever could see in town. It was truly beautiful.

Before long, the calm was broken by Jessica's voice, "I don't mean to be a party pooper, but I have to get home by my curfew or I'll be in big trouble. Can any of you see your watch? I don't have a light on mine, and it's too dark out here to read it."

Steven pushed a button on his watch that made the numbers light up.

"I have 11:45," he quietly answered.

"I have to go, Mark, really. My house is on the opposite side of town. It's gonna take at least 10-15 minutes to get there," Jessica stated as she stood.

"Sure, no problem," Mark replied.

The four of them jogged back to the car and left. It took several minutes for them just to get back to town. As the minutes flew, Jessica started getting nervous. The car was quiet and fairly dark. Steven had been sitting behind Mark the whole time. He leaned forward to look over Mark's shoulder.

"Dude, do you realize your gas light is on? How long has it been like that," Steven questioned.

Mark looked down at it and replied, "Damn, it went on when we were on the way to Suzie's house before dinner. I totally forgot. This is my dad's car, and I'm not that familiar with his lights."

"Look, there is a station up there about two blocks. I'll just put a couple dollars in to get all of us home. It won't take long. I'm sorry Jessica. I will apologize to your parents in person if I need to," Steven offered.

Jessica didn't respond. Her mind was racing, and she was trying to figure out a way to avoid getting caught. She was going to be late for curfew, and her father wouldn't tolerate that. If the alarm system was on she would have to deactivate it, and that would log her time. If the alarm system was off, she could sneak in her bedroom window and act as if she had come in earlier. If ...

Her thoughts were interrupted by Suzie's voice, "Jessica! Jessica. Do you need to use the pay phone to call your parents and let them know you are on your way?"

The car door opened and Mark got out to pump the gas.

Jessica shook her head slowly. Calling them would only alert them to the fact she knew she was running late. That would work for a lot of teenagers who had parents who trusted them. Jessica's father didn't trust her. He didn't trust anyone. Calling would make no difference to him.

"No, I'll just deal with it when I get home," Jessica replied as she felt a cold fear starting to spread through her body.

Steven put his hand on her shoulder and leaned over to whisper, "Mark is always late. I'm sorry. If I would have known sooner that you had a curfew, I would have offered to drive you myself. Mark has never had a curfew so he doesn't understand that the rest of the world doesn't necessarily live that way. Before you leave I want you to know I had a great time."

Jessica smiled at him. She wished he would have been the one to drive too. "I had a wonderful time as well."

Mark finished with the gas and got back in the car. He drove straight to Jessica's house. "Sorry Jessica. I mean it. I'd be happy to tell your parents it wasn't your fault. You told me you needed to be home by midnight. It's just seven minutes after. Hopefully, they will go easy on you and be understanding."

"Yeah, that's my dad, understanding." No

one recognized the sarcasm as Jessica got out of the car in front of her house.

She walked up the drive way and looked to see if the alarm system was on. It was. She disarmed it and went inside totally defeated.

Her father was sitting in the den in his chair. He looked at Jessica, looked up at the grandfather clock, and then looked back at Jessica.

"You irresponsible little whore! Look at you. You're dressed in that little mini skirt wanting the little high school boys to look at you. Well, did it work?" he sneered.

Instantly Jessica sized him up. He was drunk. He was already angry. She didn't like anything she saw. Should she try and explain why she was late? Where was her mother? They usually waited up together. What should be her next move? Maybe he wouldn't do anything to her if she could calm him down.

"Dad," she started. "Please, just listen. It wasn't my fault I'm late. He was low on gas and had to stop." Jessica tried to reason with him.

"I don't give a shit about your excuses. You were late. Not a few seconds late, but almost ten whole minutes late! Do you know you look like a slut dressed like that? Why would you leave my house and look like that, and then have no regard for my rules whatsoever. Who do you think you are? Huh? Answer me!" he angrily demanded.

Jessica's voice started to quiver, "Where's mom?"

Mr. Taylor got up out of his chair and screamed, "Your mom? Your mom is out with her friends tonight. Ladies Night Out!" he mocked. "It must be in the air that Taylor women dress up like whores and let the whole town see how slutty they are. Isn't that right?"

Jessica didn't like where this was going. She turned to go to her room and try to avoid her father. That's what her mother had advised. When he was on a rampage, avoid him the best you could. She avoided his derogatory comments and tried to stay calm.

"I'm just going to go to bed. Let's talk tomorrow instead," Jessica said over her shoulder.

She started off down the hallway; her plan was to lock herself in her room before he could get to her. Shaking the whole way, she quickened her pace but didn't want to run. She was afraid if she ran he would see it as a sign of rebellion and attack her. She was halfway down the hallway when she heard his heavy breathing behind her. She walked even faster. As she reached her doorway, her father's violent hands grabbed her from behind and threw her onto her bed.

"No!" Jessica screamed in terror, but that didn't stop him.

Like a savage, he tore her shirt exposing her bra. He leered at her exposed flesh.

"Is this what you wanted, you little whore? That's why you wore it, isn't it? Isn't it?" He mocked her as his eyes greedily drank in her flesh like he did his favorite booze.

Everything about him repulsed her -- the way his body reeked of sweat and alcohol, the way his breath reeked of stale smoke and alcohol, his loud breathing. Jessica thought she was going to throw up. This couldn't be happening. He used his size and strength to render her helpless. Like always, she couldn't do anything to stop him. She was paralyzed. Cries of humiliation filled her bedroom. The walls cried with her.

He raised his open hand back and slapped Jessica across the face busting her top lip. Blood started oozing down into her mouth. She could taste it. His filthy hands touched her and violated any boundaries she had. He kissed her neck while he talked to her.

He blamed her, "You realize this is all your fault. You have been asking for this a long time," Mr. Taylor justified.

Jessica remained silent. She didn't know if she could take this much longer. She tried to disconnect her mind and think about the evening. She changed her focus when she realized she had been wearing that skirt. She wanted Steven to think she was pretty, that's all. She didn't want this kind of attention! Her father kept pawing at her clothing, trying to reveal more of her.

Every muscle in her body tightened. She wanted to be anywhere but here. She would rather take her own life than to be here! How could she make it stop? That's all she wanted. 'Dear Lord,' she started to pray in her mind, 'please make him go away. Make him leave me alone. I'm sorry if I caused this. I just want it to stop. I'll do anything to make it stop. Please. Please.' She wasn't sure, but the last "please" directed at God may have been audible.

A yell coming from the end of the hallway made time stand still, "Honey, I'm home!! Woo hoo! Girl's Night Out is over!"

It was a miracle. Her mother was home! Her father jumped to his feet, grabbed at his pants, and clumsily zipped them back up. He left his shirt unbuttoned as he hurried into Jessica's bathroom. He must have buttoned his shirt while in there. He flushed the toilet and cleared his throat.

"Here I am. I was just using Jessica's bathroom 'cause it was closer to the TV. How was your night?" His voice trailed off as he walked toward the front of the house.

Jessica's body was trembling, but she managed to get to her feet. She quietly shut her door and found a box of old yearbooks in her closet. The box was extremely heavy, but she managed to push it along the floor until it sat next to her bedroom door. She also grabbed the chair that sat at her desk and wedged it under the door handle. Then she entered her bathroom from the door that connected to her room and walked over to the opposite door. The second door lead to the hallway. She locked it. No one was going to get to her again tonight.

She collapsed on her bed and began to sob. Life couldn't get any worse. Her father's attacks were getting more sexually aggressive, and she had recently told the only person who tried to help her that she never wanted to see him again. She felt more alone than ever. The weight of the world seemed to be resting on her shoulders, and her shoulders couldn't take much more.

When Jessica finally fell asleep Aaron was the only thing on her mind.

She was back at the beach. Waves were crashing against the rocks that lined the shore. Aaron was walking toward her from

126

the opposite direction. As he got closer his smile faded; her memories entered his mind. He watched in horror, and he shook his head.

"Jessica, my sweet Jessica. Words can't tell you how sorry I am."

Tears started welling up in his eyes. It was obvious her attack deeply touched him. He continued, "I can't let you do this anymore. Please listen to me. Please, you have to get help."

Jessica's tears were still flowing down her cheeks as she defended her previous decision. "I can't Aaron. What if I tell the counselor or a teacher and it's reported to authorities? Then the authorities come and take me out of the home, but for some reason they have to send me back. I'm afraid he will do more. I just want him to stop. I don't want him to go to jail. I don't want anyone to even know about this. I just want him to stop that's all."

"Jesse, why can't you see he is not just going to stop? Someone is going to have to stop him -- someone who has more power than you or me." Aaron put his arms around her and just held her. Jessica continued to cry in his arms. She felt safe with him.

"You know," she changed the subject, "that I didn't mean it when I said I never wanted to see you again. You are the only one I have ever loved."

"I know, and you are the only one I have ever truly loved. That is why you have to get help. I know you don't want to, but if you won't do it for yourself, will you do it for me? The steps you will have to go through after you tell someone can't be as bad as what you are going through now. And what about the next time? And the next? He won't stop no matter how bad you wish him to. He damn near raped you tonight. What if your mom doesn't come home next time? What if he rapes you, then you get pregnant? Telling someone your story can't be worse than that." His voice quivered. Jessica could tell it was painful for him to see her like this. He went on to say, "I don't know if I can take seeing this happen to you again."

"I promise to think about it." She said, "I will look into my options when we go to school Monday." They sat holding one another quietly, peacefully. In his arms, Jessica was safe. That's all she wanted right now.

She looked up at Aaron and started to speak. He had a strange look on his face. It startled Jessica. He started to let out a moan, but it barely could be heard. Jessica released her grip to get a better look at him. Something was wrong. He was shaking his head back and forth like he couldn't see very well. He kept blinking his eyes in order to refocus. Then his right arm started to disappear. One second you could see it, and then it transitioned into a cloud-like substance and faded away closely followed by part of the right side of his body. A shadowy looking red liquid started trickling down from the left side of his mouth. He looked as though he were going to pass out. He cried out, "Jessica! It hurts. I ... I can't... oh, God it hurts so bad!"

His body continued to disappear slowly. He was leaving the dream. "Jessica, I love you. I have to go .... " Words were no longer coming from his mouth. Jessica started to scream in horror.

"Aaron! Aaron! What's happening? She grabbed at where his body was still standing, but her hand went right through him. She was grabbing at air. His eyes were closing slowly as he was fading.

Jessica continued to scream, "Help! Can anyone help me!!! Aaron don't leave! What's happening? Talk to me! Tell me what's happening to you? Don't leave me Aaron! Please, God, please don't let him leave!"

As the last word escaped her breath, Aaron vanished from the dream for good. Jessica collapsed on the sand clutching her face and crying -- crying and screaming, "NOOOOOOOOOOO! You can't leave me, Aaron. I need you!" Her cries were drowned out by the crash of the waves.

Jessica sat straight up in her bed. Her cheeks were still wet from crying. Her heart was still racing. Her throat hurt. She looked at the clock which read 2:45 a.m. Her chest was heavy. Sadness blanketed her. She had to find Aaron first thing in the morning so she could see if he had had the same dream. No, this was no dream; it was nightmare. She had to see why he disappeared on her like that – especially when she needed him the most. She had to make sure he was okay.

Chapter 9

The Final Dream

Jessica awoke at 7:45 a.m. with no alarm. Today was Saturday, her mind traveled to the first Saturday she mustered up the courage to show him the necklace. She wished she had a meeting planned with Aaron this morning, but she didn't.

She looked around her room. The chair and box still blocked her door. Jessica was relieved. She pulled the blankets back to discover that she was still wearing the clothes from last night. She ripped them off as fast as she could. Jessica didn't want them to touch her any longer. She would never ever wear them again so she threw them in her trash can.

Jessica walked quietly into her bathroom and turned the water in her shower on to heat it up. Glancing at the door to the hallway, she assured herself that the door was still locked. When the mirror started to fog up, she opened the glass door to her shower and stepped in. She had a little waterproof radio that hung from the shower head. She reached up and turned it on. The radio was set to her favorite local station. She started washing her hair listening to a Madonna song. "You may be my lucky star, but I'm the luck-i-est by far...." She had just rinsed the shampoo out and was adding conditioner when the song ended. The disc jockey's voice broke in, "Good morning everyone. I hope your Saturday morning is off to a great start as you're listening to the latest hits on KJ103. I'm Dawn Michelle with your weekend update. We are starting off the morning with sad news. There was a single car accident around three o'clock in the morning on Highway 51 west of Stillwater. The driver of the 1979 Ford Fairmont apparently lost control and swerved off the road striking a tree. The driver was hospitalized with multiple injuries; the passenger was thrown from the car and was pronounced dead at the scene. Investigators believe alcohol was involved, and neither passenger was wearing a seat belt. Names are being withheld until family is notified. We are told both the driver and passenger were minors. Our next story in the news takes us to…."

Jessica turned it off. She didn't want to hear anymore. She finished rinsing the conditioner out of her hair and got out of the shower. She dressed as quickly as she could in sweatpants and sweatshirt. She towel dried her hair and ran a wide toothed comb through it. She grabbed her keys and billfold, unlocked the bathroom door, and left. She didn't like the feeling that was hovering over her. She had to see Aaron.

She drove in a state of numbness to his house. So much had happened in the last 24 hours. As she pulled onto his street, her stomach tightened. She saw cars -- many, many cars -- parked all around Aaron's house. Jessica couldn't seem to comprehend everything she was seeing. She parked her car and without emotion approached the house. Instead of the silence she heard the last time she was there, she heard voices coming from inside. She knocked on the door. An older woman opened it. Her eyes were red and swollen. Jessica stared at her trying to read the expression written on her face.

In a low voice the lady replied, "You must be one of A.J.'s friends. Come on in, dear." Jessica felt uneasy but she had to go.

Silently she stepped into the house. To her right was a room full of people. They were older people. Some cried, some stared off into space, others tried carrying on conversations. Jessica spotted Aaron's mother, the lady who had opened the door for her that first Saturday. His mother was crying into a fist full of tissues.   Aaron's father, the man she recognized from the school incident, stood behind his wife with his hands on both her shoulders. His eyes were bloodshot, too.

Jessica's knees started to feel weak. The air she was breathing seemed so thick and suffocating. Pleading for an explanation, Jessica made eye-contact with the woman who let her into the house moments ago.

The woman put her arm around Jessica, "Are you okay? You look pale."

Jessica gathered every ounce of energy she had to force the words out of her mouth. "Where is Aaron? I need to see Aaron."

"Oh dear," the woman gasped, "You don't know?"

Tears were welling up and her throat was constricting. She insisted again, "I've got to talk to Aaron. It's very important."

The tears started rolling down Jessica's cheeks one by one, creating little rivulets that traced her nose and the outer edge of her quivering lips to pool together at her chin and fall unnoticed. Her body knew what her mind was not accepting.

"I'm sorry to be the one to have to tell you.

I'm his aunt. He was killed in a car wreck this morning."

Jessica persisted, "Are they sure it was him? I need to speak to him. You don't understand. He was going to help me."

That was all she could say before breaking down. Her heart was broken. She turned to leave this place – this place and the pain were consuming her. The tears blurred her vision as she made her way to the door. Aaron's aunt followed her and said she needed to sit down because she looked pale. Jessica instead fled to the safety of her car and drove to Hidden Park. Maybe Aaron was there. Maybe they were all wrong.

She pulled her car into the alley entrance and parked on the grass. The flood of tears poured from her soul. She stumbled over to the picnic table and lay her head across the very spot she saw Aaron lay his head one day. The only sounds in the park came from her whimpering. It was as though the birds were paying tribute by silencing their songs. The wind no longer danced. The sun no longer smiled. Aaron was gone. She pleaded one last time to the empty park, "Aaron please, please come back. I can't do this alone. I need your help." Crying her words she said again, "I need your help."

Jessica must have sat there an hour before she left. She drove home emotionally exhausted. Her mother was just waking up when she saw Jessica come in the front door.

"Jessica, what is wrong?" Her mom asked.

"Everything," she said in a soft and defeated voice." "Everything."

"Oh surely it can't be that bad," her mom reasoned.

Jessica looked her mother in the eyes and said, "He's dead. One of my friends was killed in a car wreck last night, well early this morning actually."

Her mother came up to her and hugged her. "I'm so sorry. It's hard when someone your own age dies. It seems so unnecessary."

"I just want to go to my room and be alone right now," Jessica mumbled as she shrugged off her mother's embrace.

Jessica started down the hallway. Forgetting she had barricaded her door shut, she turned the knob and tried to open it. Of course, it banged against the chair and box on the other side. She shook her head and walked through her bathroom. That's all she needed was a reminder of last night.

Her hair was still wet when she crawled back in bed. She didn't care. Nothing mattered any more anyway. Her thoughts were all over the place. One minute she was remembering Aaron and their dreams, the next she was thinking about Steven, her blind date. Unfortunately, she would revisit the horror with her father, too. Should she tell? She didn't know. All she knew was one day her world was somewhat normal and the next day it was crumbling around her. She didn't care about anything right now. She fell into a restless slumber.

She was at the picnic table at Hidden Park. Sitting alone. She got up and walked toward the swings but decided instead to lie on the teeter-totter. She looked up into the sky. Sparrows skirted around the clouds with not a care in the world. Cardinals and blue jays joined in the flight at times too. The birds were free. She admired that. She longed for the day she would be free.

A noise shook her from her thoughts and she sat back up. It was Aaron. Smiling the most glorious smile, he was standing right beside her. He looked so happy, so alive!

His voice filled the air, "You don't need to cry for me anymore, Jesse. I'm free. Just like the birds you were watching. I am finally free."

Jessica jumped to her feet and said, "I thought you were dead!" She reached out to hug him.

He put his hand out to stop her. "You can't. This is not my physical body anymore. It's just the image of my physical body so you would recognize me and not be afraid. I have come to explain what happened and to guide you in the direction you must go."

As Jessica looked at him more carefully she could tell something was different. He looked like he wasn't quite solid. She struggled with a description in her mind. It was as though she could see him, yet see through him at the same time.

Aaron began, "Friday night I was at a party with all my friends. We were drinking pretty heavily and having a good time. Before I knew it, Ronda told me she had to go home. Since I rode with her, I had to leave with her, too. We were driving down a back country *road at first, and I started feeling sick. I climbed in the back seat of her car and must have fallen asleep. The next thing I was aware of was our dream. We were at the beach. That is where I lived before I moved to Stillwater.*

Without warning the dream faded to black. I could hear you, but couldn't see you. I started feeling a horrible pain in my right side. When I awoke, I could see men in uniform all around me talking to each other about my injuries. They said I had been thrown from the car when Ronda hit a tree. I had massive head trauma. I wanted to tell them I could hear them, but my words were trapped inside. Everything went black again. This time I woke up and was in a place totally unknown to me. It was like an empty room with no windows or doors. I felt a peace come over me. Then I was filled with a presence of overwhelming love. You know how you and I could see each other's memories? Well, I saw into God's eyes. This incredibly detailed knowledge of the human race filled my mind. It showed me that we are all connected in some way to God. Our societies are so simple minded when it comes to defining who He is. He's beyond definition. The only way I can think of explaining it is He masterminded everything in the universe. He is beyond everything we have ever known.

Well, God granted me the favor of being able to speak to you one more time. He sees your pain, Jesse. He hurts when you hurt, but He's always there if you need to talk. My job now is to tell you only what you need to know. My promise to you has always been to help you however I could. I have some information, but it is up to you to figure some things out on your own." Aaron paused and smiled at Jessica before continuing, "First to fully understand our situation you need to research the following dates: January 23, 1945, and November 22, 1966. Let the inner voice of your soul guide you, and you will understand."

"But Aaron..." Jessica tried to interrupt.

"Second, you have to stop kidding yourself about your father. It will get worse if you don't do something. There are good people out there who would do anything to help you. There are women who have gone down the same painful path, but who are now on the other side to help. Again, listen to your soul. Your instincts will guide you, and you will find the right person to tell. But you have to find the courage to tell someone!"

"Aaron wait ... I told you," Jessica tried to get him to stop and listen.

"Third, I am not dead. I am still the same soul I always was. Death is simply a time of transition and learning. My new transformation will take place at the right time when everything is in alignment."

"Alignment? What alignment? Aaron what are you talking about?" Jessica cried.

"And last, I love you with all my heart. I have always loved you. Even if you live to be 100 years old in this lifetime, it is just a blink of an eye compared to eternity. Jesse, we

have an eternity," Aaron finished.

He stepped forward and leaned over to kiss her cheek; Jessica felt a tiny breeze across her face. As the air caressed her skin it had a calming effect. She thought she could feel his lips, but she wasn't for sure. As soon as he pulled his head back, he looked into her eyes, winked, then vanished. Jessica never was able to say what she wanted to say, but she was so glad to see Aaron again.

Chapter 10

Discovery

Jessica awoke immediately. As soon as her eyes shot open, she jumped off her bed to look for a piece of paper and something to write with. She scribbled down the two dates he had given her. Then she closed her eyes and tried to replay exactly what he had said. He said that (1)God was Universal Love; (2) she would figure out their relationship with those dates; (3) she needed to look for someone to tell about her father; and,(4) he would transform when everything was "aligned." She jotted a few key words down so she would remember all that he said.

'Hmmmm,' Jessica thought to herself. She had always believed in God so that wasn't surprising. It did comfort her to know that Aaron was *with* God. She understood the part about telling someone. Aaron had been pleading with her for some time now to do just that. She would worry about that one later. The whole "transforming" thing was a total mystery. She had no idea what he was talking about there, but the dates ... she should look up those dates and see what he was talking about. That is where she should begin unraveling this mystery.

Her hair was dry now. She didn't feel like fixing it so she just braided it quickly and put on a visor. She found her car keys and purse. As she was leaving, she yelled into the main part of the house, "I'm going to the public library. I'll be back later."

Her mother answered back, "Okay. Be careful!"

She didn't see or hear her father. That was fine with her!

Once at the library, she went row by row looking at anything that would catch her attention. Finally after a while she started feeling as though she were wasting time, so she went to one of the "help" desks. There were several people working. She approached the desk manned by a middle-aged woman. The woman had a smile on her face and seemed to enjoy her job a great deal.

"Excuse me," Jessica said to her politely.

"Yes, ma'am. How can I assist you today?" the lady answered.

Jessica began, "Where would I need to go if I were looking up particular dates."

"That depends. What are you looking for with those dates? Are you looking for something that occurred worldwide that might be found in history book or encyclopedia? Or are you just concerned with something that took place at a local level?" the librarian asked to get a better idea which direction to send the girl.

Jessica didn't know. Aaron had said to follow her inner voice, but her inner voice apparently had laryngitis. She didn't hear anything.

"I'm not sure. Can you tell me about each of them?" Jessica inquired.

"Well, if you want to know something that occurred that might be found in a history book somewhere, you would go into that room over there." The lady pointed over Jessica's right shoulder and continued, "If it is something that just occurred in everyday life, you may want to scan the archived newspapers. Those are found in this room behind me."

Jessica got goose bumps when the lady said "everyday life." Her instinct told her that is where she should look. The lady opened the door for her. Jessica walked in. A couple of machines sat in the center of the room surrounded by walls lined with large filing cabinets. She walked over and looked at their labels. There were newspapers from all across the United States: *The Daily Oklahoman*, *The Denver Post*, *Los Angeles Times*, *Miami Herald*, and so on. She thought she would start with the local newspaper, *The Stillwater Newspress*. She went to the filing cabinet drawers that held that newspaper. When she opened the drawer, little cylinder containers sat inside with labels on the lid revealing the dates. She picked up the one that included January of 1945. She opened the cylinder and saw a rolled up piece of film. The film had to be threaded through one of the machines in the center of the room. Once the film was in place, there were buttons on the machine that controlled how fast she could scan the paper. She sat at the machine as though it were a desk. The flat table top had a screen-like area where images of the newspaper would appear to be scanned. It was like watching a movie, only the images were pictures of what each page of the newspaper looked like. Jessica could zoom in or zoom out on the image to change the size of the image.

Jessica kept turning the knob to move the pages of the newspaper along. She scanned the headlines keeping an open mind. It took a while to get to the 23rd but she was finally there. Page after page, story after story she kept searching for something that would trigger a gut feeling. It was hard to search for the unknown. When she finished that day's newspaper she returned the film to its container and got up to find a different newspaper. 'Think, think, think,' she said to herself. There was no way she could spend that much time on each one. She didn't know which paper to search next. She remembered that Aaron told her he lived on a beach before he moved to Stillwater. Perhaps that was a clue.

Jessica ran her hands across each of the file cabinet drawers hoping to "feel" something. She felt overwhelmed. How was she going to find what she needed? Her eyes looked back and forth at all the titles. She noticed that her eyes kept coming back to the Miami Herald. For some reason, she was drawn to that paper. It was such a big paper compared to her hometown newspaper. She pulled open the drawer with a little bit of dread. It would take a while to read through this one.

She took the film out and threaded it through the machine. She turned and adjusted all the knobs, and found January 23, 1945. Flipping through page by page without knowing what she was looking for was tedious. She had been in the room an hour now and was only on her second paper. Finally something caught her eye. In the "Lifestyle" section, she noticed the birth announcements. There were two that jumped off the page at her. The first one read:

Girl, Jessica Ann Torinadi; 6 lbs 3 oz; born to Eddie and Staci Torinadi of Miami Beach.

Three announcements down she read:

Boy, Aaron James; 7 lbs 11 oz; born to Quinn and Kristi Huffington of South Miami.

A chill shot down her spine. This was it. There were small pieces of rectangular shaped papers stacked in a little card board box that looked like the lid to something. Along with the paper were little sharpened pencils about 3 inches long -- the kind of pencils that could sharpened on either end. Jessica grabbed one of each and scribbled down the two birth announcements. She returned the film to its container and looked for the other date: November 22, 1966. She decided to stay with the same newspaper.

Another hour passed as Jessica scanned page after page. She read about NASA's Gemini 12 flight, about a guy who caught a record breaking fish, about local celebrations. Suddenly a chill hit her body as she read the headline, "Vietnam Veteran and Fiancé' Murdered on Wedding Day." Her eyes couldn't help but to read the article: "The bride, Ms. Jessica Ann Tornadi, and the groom, Third class Navy Corpsman Aaron James Huffington, were brutally gunned down when an anti-Vietnam War protestor entered the church. Investigators on the scene said the protestor knew that Huffington had served in Vietnam, but did not know Huffington's roll as a war hero. Huffington's job in the war was to tend to the wounded. He was shot when his platoon was attacked by the North Vietnamese." Jessica was stunned to read further, "Huffington had been back in the United States only months before his wedding. Jessica Ann Torinadi was a senior at the University of Oklahoma studying Elementary Education. The couple planned to live in Oklahoma until she finished her degree. The gunman escaped as wedding guests watched in

143

horror. Funeral arrangements are pending."

She sat there frozen. The murder had occurred in the year before her birth. Aaron's words crept into her head, "to understand our situation..." and, "Jesse, we have an eternity."

Like pieces of a puzzle, things were starting to fit together. Her thoughts ventured back to what Aaron had told her about his grandmother. How did she know they were destined to be together? How did she know they had been together before, and their souls were going to search for each other in the night? Regardless, she had been right. They were definitely soul mates. But now what?

"Honey, the library is about to close. Do you need my help with anything?" It was the same sweet middle-aged woman who had helped her before.

"No thank you, I found exactly what I was looking for." Jessica put everything back the way it was, snatched up her piece of paper, and left. She sat in her parked car just watching people walk by. Her mind needed time to absorb everything. She had never considered being linked to someone for eternity. Did that mean she and Aaron had more lives together? If that were the case, it went against everything she had ever learned in church. You die, go to Heaven, and spend eternity there, not here. This made her question everything.

Jessica left the parking lot and started driving home. The closer to home she was, the more distant her discovery at the library seemed -- the less believable it became. When she arrived home, she just went straight to her room and avoided eye contact with her mother and her father. She distanced herself from the rest of the world --

physically and emotionally. She had nothing left in her. She stayed in her room the rest of the night.

Sunday morning while the Taylors attended church, Aaron was laid to rest in a small gravesite service with only family present. Jessica was still angry at God, so she refused to pray or sing when everyone else did. On the way home from church, her father wanted to stop for a bite to eat, so they did. Throughout the meal Jessica just sat in a weepy daze. Her parents voiced their concern, but she said she was fine. Her parents respectfully left her alone.

In the afternoon, Jessica tried to finish any homework she had. About 5:30 she had the strong desire to be near Aaron. She had the idea to visit his grave. So she silently left the house in her car. She drove to the cemetery where she knew he had been laid to rest earlier in the day. It was a small cemetery south of town called Sunrise Memorial. Jessica pulled her car into a parking spot, sat for a moment, then opened her door to step out of the car.

The sun was going down and a light breeze blew stray leaves haphazardly around. She looked for a freshly dug plot. She found it right away. As she approached the grave, the turmoil inside her calmed down. A song came into her mind the moment she found Aaron's headstone. It was the song "*Faithfully*," by the band Journey. She had the feeling that Aaron's spirit was there, telling her that he was "forever yours, faithfully." She could hear the song clearly in her mind. She closed her eyes and sat next to his grave. Tears streamed down her cheeks. She didn't want him to be gone. She finally found the one for her, and now he was gone.

Life just didn't seem fair. She opened her eyes and looked up to the heavens and yelled at God. "I'm angry at you! I don't understand how you can be so loving yet you let me hurt so bad! I don't understand it at all. What did I do to deserve this? Are you punishing me? All I wanted was our 'happily ever after.' That's all. I don't know why that's so hard! God, why? Why did you take him from me? Aaron, can you even hear me? I just wanted our 'happily ever after.' I wanted that with you." She sat holding his headstone and sobbing.

When darkness blanketed the area, she knew she needed to get home. She slowly walked over to her car, got in, and drove home in silence.

Monday morning arrived and she headed to school as usual. There were counselors all over the place. Apparently, Aaron's death stirred up a lot of attention. The counselors came from all over the city. They addressed the whole student body and explained the stages of grief. The atmosphere was very solemn. They said they were "on call" all week if anyone wanted to visit with them.

Jessica had been on such an emotional roller coaster the last week that she felt empty inside today. She looked around at all the people crying -- people from all different backgrounds. There were athletes, geeks, socialites, as well as druggies. It seemed strange to her that people who wouldn't give him the time of day were crying. She started to get angry then she realized how she must appear to others. She never socialized with him either. They probably thought she was being extremely insensitive to sit there lost in her own thoughts. They had no idea.

When they were released from the

auditorium, Jessica's withdrawal continued. Suzie had tried to talk to her about lunch plans, but Jessica told her she needed her space. She found her way to the library. Alone. That's all she craved was to be alone. She found a two- seater couch on the perimeter. Plopping her books on the sofa, she sat down beside them.

Jessica considered doing something she had never done before. She thought about skipping out of her 4th period class. It was her anatomy class. She didn't' feel like dealing with that old bat of a teacher anyway. Jessica looked around. No one seemed to care. She decided to look for a book to read, something to pass the time.

Jessica was in the non-fiction section looking at books on abuse. Barely above her eye level, a ection on child abuse caught her attention. She dared not pick one of the books up thought for fear that someone might suspect something, but she was curious. She was reading the titles when a voice startled her.

"Ms. Taylor? Shouldn't you be in class?" It was Mrs. Willingham.

Embarrassed about being in front of the section on child abuse as well as getting caught skipping class, Jessica's response was soft and hoarse, "Yes, ma'am."

Sensing that Jessica might want to talk, Mrs. Willingham continued, "I love reading about human behavior, too."

It did make sense that Mrs. Willingham, of all teachers, would be in the library. After all literature and writing was her life, but why now?

"Don't you have class right now, too?" Jessica

147

smiled making sure she sounded respectful.

The teacher explained, "Oh, this is my planning period. I almost always come to the library during this time. Books have always been a nice escape for me. They seem to always be around and are written on all topics known to mankind. It reminds me that I'm not alone in this universe of ours. There is always a book written on whatever subject I need. What about you Ms. Taylor? What brings you here today?"

So many thoughts swirled around in her mind; she really just wanted to be alone. Mrs. Willingham persisted, "I have noticed changes in you that have made me worry about you. Are you doing okay?"

Jessica's nerves were shot; her emotions had been all out of whack since her father's attack, the dream, the death, the counselors' advice on grief, the secret romance, and the contradictory thoughts on life after death. She didn't know where to begin. For reasons beyond her control, she began to tear up. Mrs. Willingham observed the reaction.

"Would you like to come in my classroom? It's a little more private there. You can cry all you want to and no one has to know."

Jessica shrugged and then nodded her head. If she spoke, she knew the dam would burst, and she wouldn't be able to stop the tears. She silently picked up her books and followed Mrs. Willingham to her classroom.

Mrs. Willingham picked up one of the student chairs and carried it right up to her desk and motion for Jessica to sit down. Jessica didn't know what she would say, if anything.

Mrs. Willingham comforted her and said, "You don't have to say anything if you don't want to. I just wanted you to have a safe place to let your emotions out, and if you want to talk, I'm here. You know I have three grown children, and I can spot a hurting child a mile away."

Jessica thought about what she said. It was nice of her not to force Jessica to talk. Of course, she was still mad about her sending the note home to her parents. She decided to divert her attention to that, "I do have a question. Why did you send that note to my parents earlier in the school year instead of just talking to me?"

Mrs. Willingham looked puzzled for a second then remembered, "Oh, that. Every three weeks I send out progress reports. I have over a hundred students a day and don't have time to counsel each one on missing work, so that is my way of keeping open lines of communication with parents. That way parents aren't surprised by the letter grade on a report card. Its purpose is to get parents and students to communicate more. "

"Oh," was all Jessica said.

Mrs. Willingham looked right at Jessica, "I've been doing this a long time. I may have strict rules, but they were created with the students' best interests in mind. Sometimes they work and sometimes they don't. I just do the best I can." She smiled.

Jessica smiled back -- sadly.

"Jessica, I have watched you all year long. I know you are devastated by the loss of your classmate. But I have to be honest with you, that's not why I think you are so sad." She stopped right there.

"What do you mean?" Jessica asked.

"Let's just say I worry about you. I'm not sure what is going on in your world, but you show signs of quite a bit of stress. Just know that if you want to talk, I'm a good listener. I love my job, and I believe there is more to it than teaching. I'm here to take care of my students too." She reached out and gave Jessica a warm, motherly hug.

Jessica needed that. She had needed that for a long time. She never had the courage to speak up that day and tell Mrs. Willingham everything, but she left knowing that when she did find the courage, she could come back.

Chapter 11

The Call

Jessica kept to herself for several days. She had distanced herself from Suzie, from the rest of the cheerleaders, from her mother, and, especially, from her father. She had a thought about Aaron's lifeless body in a casket. He was put in the ground and covered with dirt. It just didn't seem right. Life didn't seem right. To top everything off, she never had another dream of Aaron.

Since Aaron's last visit, Jessica had watched Mrs. Willingham with a combination of hope and suspicion. Could she trust her? Her gut told her yes, but her fears told her no. Besides, even if she told her, then what was next? That's what really scared her. She didn't want to make a scene. She didn't want her father arrested, letting everyone know her ugly secret. She didn't want to testify in court if charges were brought up. She was afraid that if she started the balling rolling and something fell through, she would be right back in his house with him. If that happened, he would really beat her. It would be ten times worse because he would be so mad that she humiliated him. It was too complicated to tell.

By the end of the week she decided on a plan designed to help her find out more information without actually revealing her secret. On Thursday, at the end of her first hour class, she asked Mrs. Willingham if she could talk to her during her planning period. Mrs. Willingham said, "Sure," and issued Jessica a pass.

Her second and third hour classes seemed to drag on, but that gave her time to rehearse in her mind what she was going to say. She was only on a fact finding mission, nothing more. The bell to dismiss them from the students' third hour class finally rang. Jessica went straight to Mrs. Willingham's room. Students were slowly walking out. As soon as the room cleared, Mrs. Willingham motioned her to come in.

Jessica sat on one of the front row seats and watched Mrs. Willingham sit back down at her desk. "What can I help you with Jessica?" she inquired.

Jessica, as rehearsed in her head, said, "Well, I need some information. I have a cousin ... who lives in another town ... who is going through a really tough time. Her step-father does things to her. She knows that if she told, he would probably get in big trouble, so she is afraid to tell. She just wants him to stop. She doesn't want him to go to jail. What should I tell her to do?"

"For starters, replied Mrs. Willingham, "I want to congratulate you on being such a great cousin to find out this information for her. It takes a special soul to reach out and help others. Secondly, how old is your cousin and what state does she live in?"

"Why? Does that matter?" Jessica asked a little suspiciously.

"Well, each state is a little different on how they work with domestic violence where children are involved. Plus, it is handled a little differently for younger children compared to older children," Mrs. Willingham patiently explained.

Jessica told her, "She is 17 years old, and she lives here in Oklahoma."

"Also, are you talking physical abuse or sexual abuse?" Mrs. Willingham asked.

"Bo...." Jessica had to clear her throat before finally saying, "Both."

"Okay, here is what you need to tell her." Mrs. Willingham opened her drawer and pulled out what looked like a business card and handed it to Jessica. "If she feels she is in **immediate** danger she needs to call 911. Her safety is of the utmost importance. If it is more of a preventative action, she needs to find an adult she can talk to -- like a school counselor or a teacher, if she can't tell another family member. Here I am going to put my phone number on the back. She has my permission to call me if she needs someone to help her through the process. If she prefers to deal with a stranger she can call the number listed here. It will tell her the closest 'safe place.' A safe place is a company that has agreed to train employees on sheltering kids who need somewhere to be safe. She will need to get to one of them. Each location has at least one person who is trained to get her to the next step."

Jessica interrupted, "So she needs to tell someone, either 911, a counselor, or teacher, or one of these 'safe place' people."

"That's exactly right. Your poor cousin shouldn't have to go this alone. No one should. There are plenty of adults who are trained to handle crises just like this. After telling someone, she will most likely be transferred to the Payne County Youth Shelter. She will stay there until a decision is made on her safety. It could be as simple as making her step-father go through counseling himself before he is allowed to see her again, or if it is serious, she may be moved into foster care in another city while the officials take care of her step-father. I know I'm not giving you exact answers Jessica, which is why she needs to tell someone. She will need guidance through the entire process, and each person's process is a little different," Mrs. Willingham explained.

"Mrs. Willingham, if you don't mind me asking, why do you know so much about this?" Jessica quietly inquired.

Mrs. Willingham took a second to collect her words. "Just tell your cousin I have been there. I got into teaching because I love kids and wanted to help all those who were just like me. It's funny how so many people think high school students are just like adults. The reality is that they aren't adults. They are still kids who need adult guidance. They still need the love and attention the little kids need; they just need it in different ways," Mrs. Willingham replied softly.

"Thank you, Mrs. Willingham. I will absolutely share this with her," Jessica gathered her things and left.

She wanted to think about what Mrs. Willingham had said. She needed to plan her next move. Aaron's advice lingered in her mind. Gosh, she didn't want to tell anyone about her situation, but she knew he was right. She at least owed that to him.

The weekend was upon her before she knew it. It was funny how a whole week of life can go by without even knowing where it went. She felt like the whole time was spent thinking about different scenarios. She wished she had more control over everything. These days she felt she was in control of nothing, absolutely nothing.

Suzie called and asked her if she wanted to go shopping. Jessica said, "No." Her mother asked if she wanted to accompany her to the nail salon. Jessica said, "No." Her father asked if she wanted to go wash the cars with him, she said, "No." She just stayed in her room and watched television. She would join her parents occasionally for a meal, but the routine was merely ceremonial. She was only going through the motions. She must have read the card Mrs. Willingham gave her a hundred times, but she still didn't do anything about it.

Midweek Jessica's mother announced she was going up to visit her sister in Michigan for several days. Her sister was going to have a pre-cancerous tumor surgically removed, and Jessica's mom needed to be there. Jessica had never been close to her mother's side of the family because they lived so far away. She loved her aunt and hoped everything would turn out okay. She also worried about her mother traveling alone, but she understood it had to be done. Her father had to work, and Jesse had to go to school. There really wasn't another choice.

Her mother left as planned. Jessica's father was one of those men who couldn't even make a sandwich for himself, so she ended up doing all the cooking her mother would have done. Their conversations were short and to the point. Both were in their own little world. The following Sunday finally rolled around, and Jessica went to church alone. Her father had slept in. She didn't know if it was because her mother wasn't there to wake him or if he chose to sleep in.

When church was over, she drove home. As she walked in the front door, she could hear her father had the television blaring in the den. She could tell by the explosions – followed by cursing – that he was watching an old war movie. Jessica went straight to the kitchen to start making lunch, staying out of his way and avoiding conversation. She opened the refrigerator to search for lunch meat. The choices were sliced turkey, ham, and a little bit of leftover chicken. There were mustard and mayonnaise in the door. Then she opened one of the drawers that held the vegetables. It looked like there was a little bit of lettuce left and one last tomato. She would need to go by the grocery store later to stock up. She really wished her mother were here so she didn't have to keep up with the meals. She was caught off guard by her father standing in the doorway. Of course, he smelled of alcohol. He always drank on the weekends.

He looked at her with a blank stare and said, "So why have you stopped talking to everyone lately? You got a problem?"

"No, Dad. I just don't feel like talking." She kept her eyes locked on the top shelf of the refrigerator.

"Don't you disrespect me! I'm your father. You look at me when I'm talking to you," Mr. Taylor boomed.

Jessica froze. She didn't want to trigger an outburst from him so she blankly stared at him. It was amazing to her that in his mind it was always about him. He was always so worried about someone embarrassing *him*, ruining *his* reputation, disrespecting *him*. He never saw things from her point of view -- ever.

"Your mom is too busy with that damn sister of hers halfway across the country, and I need a sandwich. She doesn't care that I have a lot of work to do this week. She just up and left with no regard for my feelings. She does whatever the hell she wants to do. Now, how long is it going to take you to make me a turkey sandwich?" Mr. Taylor howled.

"I can have it ready in 5 minutes, Dad," Jessica answered.

"Okay then." He mumbled and returned to the den.

Minutes later she brought the sandwich to him.

"Thanks," he said. "Before you go I want you to see something." He had a strange look in his eye.

Jessica noticed he was sitting in her mother's favorite chair which was odd. He normally had his own favorite chair. His eyes were slightly bloodshot, and he had a smirk on his face. She had to be careful not to aggravate him when he had been drinking like this.

"You know I had a procedure last week. It's healing up real nicely. I had a hernia." Mr. Taylor paused as though he was waiting for Jessica to comment, but she just stared at him blankly. She froze after handing him the sandwich. He carelessly placed the plate with his freshly made sandwich on the coffee table beside the chair. It clanged when the crystal hit the wood. He raised his hand toward her and demanded, "Give me your hand."

Jessica reluctantly held out her hand. She was very confused. First of all she had never heard him talk of a hernia before today, and, secondly, she didn't know where he was going with this. Mr. Taylor took her hand. Jessica hadn't realized it, but he had unzipped his jeans. His belly was big enough to hide it. He pulled Jessica's hand down to his groin area. She was repulsed and scared at the same time. She didn't want to touch him! But he was making her. He was pulling her hand closer and closer to him. Her thoughts raced. If she pulled away, what would he do? He had been acting strange already. Would it send him into one of his violent tirades? Would he hit her or throw her against the wall? But if she didn't pull away, would he think she thought it was okay? She didn't want to touch him, why would he make her? She kept a strong tension by resisting without making it obvious. Her mind was churning wildly. She had to figure out a way to escape. Aaron's word's flashed through her mind, "He won't stop. You will have to stop him."

Her father was stronger so he forced her hand down farther. Her hand brushed the top of his jeans, and then she felt flesh. She knew in an instant what he was doing was wrong. There was no hernia; he was making her touch him inappropriately. She wanted to throw up. Barely audible, a yelp escaped her lips, "Oh God, NO!" And without thinking she jerked with all her might. Her hand broke free. It startled Mr. Taylor. Her eyes flew open wide with fear, and a flood of adrenaline shot through her body. Mr. Taylor looked confused and leaned toward her as though he were going to grab her. Jessica again surprised herself when she slapped his arms away as hard as she could and took off running toward her bedroom.

"What the hell?" Mr. Taylor roared. He jumped out of his chair and started to follow Jessica. He struggled to get his pants zipped as he went. "Where are you going?" he yelled after her. "Get back here! You disrespectful little bitch." The alcohol affected his coordination as he clumsily tried to run after her.

Jessica's heart was pounding so loud she could hear it. There was a hallway table that held everyone's keys in a decorative bowl. She made a split decision to grab both sets of keys in there. Then she grabbed her purse which she always placed on a shelf just under the tabletop. A crystal clear image of the "safe place" card shot through her mind. She knew the card was in her purse. She was shaking from head to toe. Was she really doing this?

She continued down the hallway towards her bedroom. Her bedroom had two entrances. She needed to block them both in order to slow Mr. Taylor down. She knew she still had the box of yearbooks right inside her front bedroom door from the last attack, though they had been moved back and her door stood wide open. She chose to enter the other way which was through her bathroom. All in one motion she locked that door and closed it behind her. The bathroom led directly into her bedroom. She sprinted around to the main entrance of her bedroom, slammed the door, and slid the yearbooks right up against it. As she did she caught a glimpse of him storming down the hallway right toward her. She didn't have time to prop the chair like she did before so she just laid it down between the box of yearbooks and the foot of her bed. It took up most of that space. If he tried to get through the door it would be very difficult to open. She hoped it would give her enough time to jump out the window and get to her car.

Her hands shook as she unlocked her window. As she slid it open, her father hit the door. He turned the knob and tried to force the door open. It banged against the yearbooks which slid them back into the chair. The chair was forcefully pushed into the end of Jessica's bed. Her bedroom door would only open about six inches. This infuriated Mr. Taylor, and he started to force the door open with his shoulder.

Finally her window opened. Jessica took her foot and kicked out the screen. She climbed into the frame of the window and jumped to the ground causing her ankles and feet to sting as she landed. A little off balance, she had to catch herself with her hands. In doing so the ground knocked her keys out of her grip. They flew a several feet in front of her. She scrambled to get to them as she heard Mr. Taylor's voice screaming from the house. She couldn't tell if he had gotten through the barrier or not; she just knew she had to stay focused on leaving -- and FAST.

As she picked up both sets of keys, she recognized his immediately and threw them as hard as she could in the opposite direction of her car. She then took her keys and opened her car door, still very aware of Mr. Taylor's screaming profanities at her. She didn't take time to see if he had made it into her room. She just started her car, threw it into reverse, and pealed out of the driveway. Halfway down her street she glanced in her rear view mirror. He had made his way outside and was standing in the middle of the street shaking his fist.

She had no idea what would happen to him, what would happen to her. She just drove while her mind processed the event.

The next half hour was a blur. She drove to the nearest gas station with a pay phone, and called the number on the back of her card.

"Hello, Willingham residence," came a pleasantly familiar voice.

"Mrs. Willingham, I need help. This is …. this is Jessica. I don't have much time. He might be coming after me."

"Who? Who might be coming after you?" Mrs. Willingham asked, alarmed.

"My father," Jessica quickly replied.

"Jessica, are you in danger?" Mrs. Willingham asked.

Jessica started crying, "Yes … maybe … I don't know …Mrs. Willingham, it's me, not a cousin."

"I know. Meet me at the public library. They are one of the safe places in town," Mrs. Willingham said soothingly.

It took about 15 minutes. Jessica openly spoke to Aaron in the car. "I'm doing this for you. I'm going to tell someone, Aaron. Now let's hope it turns out okay. I'm so scared. I wish you were here. Oh God, what have I done? What have I done? He'll kill me if I go back. I can't go back. Why can't my mom be here? Why did he make me touch him? I hate this. I'm scared, Aaron. I'm so scared."

Jessica met her teacher at the library. As soon as she spotted Mrs. Willingham, she ran up to her and gave her a huge hug. "I'm scared. What if I did the wrong thing?"

Mrs. Willingham led her in to the front desk and said to the clerk, "I need to see your 'safe place' person, now!"

The lady behind the desk immediately got on the phone and called another woman in a different department. Together they took Jessica to a private room. Jessica was asked, "Do you feel you would be in danger if you were to return?"

As soon as Jessica nodded her head, the lady made a couple more phone calls. Mrs. Willingham embraced her in a hug.

"I had a feeling it was you and not a cousin. I had a gut feeling it was you all along. You are brave to take this step, Jessica. Most girls can't bring themselves to do this. Most girls your age just live in a silent hell waiting to move away. You did the right thing, dear. I don't know how much of the process they will let me be around for, but I will try to be as involved as they will let me be. Know that if there comes a time I'm not there, it is because they won't allow it, and not because I don't care about you." Mrs. Willingham explained.

"Okay," was all Jessica could say through her tears.

The next thing Jessica knew a woman from the Payne County Child Protective Services showed up. She explained to Jessica that she was taking her to a secret location for her own protection. Jessica agreed. She couldn't go home now. She asked Jessica if there was anything she needed to get out of her car before they left since the car would be turned back over to her parents. Jessica went over and looked. She grabbed some gum, a pair of shorts and a t-shirt from the back seat. That's all she had in there.

The lady's name was Matuschka. She seemed very nice and spoke to Jessica in a soft voice. She explained how they were going to this secret location so Jessica could tell her story once, and only once. She said there would be some other specialists in this area who would be involved. Jessica was amazed at how many adults knew about child abuse.

It took them about thirty minutes to make it to the house in the country. There were no other houses around, but three other cars were already parked in front. She walked up to the front porch with Matuschka. It looked like a little old farm house, but it became quickly obvious that it had special things for added protection. There was a surveillance camera mounted on the front porch. Matuschka had to swipe an ID badge to unlock the door. The windows had a protective covering on them so no one could see in the house but the inhabitants could see out.

As soon as they entered, Jessica met an undercover policeman, a social worker, and a psychologist. She was a little bit overwhelmed. They all greeted her warmly though. The psychologist lead her into a room that looked like a living room and game room combined. There was a pool table behind an oversized sofa. A very expensive looking television sat inside one of a solid oak home entertainment center which also held a VCR and a game system. There was a deck of Uno cards on one of the coffee tables and packages of play-dough and clay on another. A wicker basket next to the table held several dolls. The paintings on the lavender walls were brightly colored. The room came alive with excitement. That room had the immediate effect it was meant to have – comfort, peace, and happiness.

As she took in the contents of the room, it occurred to Jessica that the presence of toys meant that the room needed to be equipped for very young children, like toddlers, to tell their stories – just as Jessica was there to do. The thought of younger children being abused turned her stomach. She realized she wasn't the only kid with issues. She wondered if the others who had been there before her had been forced to do things they didn't want to do like she had been. Were they hit like she had been? Or were they called horrible names like she had been? A lot of kids must come here, she thought by the looks of it -- kids who must have suffered as she had or maybe worse.

The psychologist motioned for her to sit on the couch and get comfortable. She gave Jessica the choice to visit now or to have some time alone first. Jessica had already made the decision to talk so she agreed to go first. The other members of this team would wait in the front room while they visited. Matuschka told Jessica that she was proud of her. Jessica smiled, but truth be told, she was embarrassed. She started having doubts about how bad her situation really was. She told herself, "It's not like he was going to kill me or anything, and I was only afraid he was going to rape me. He never did."

The psychologist explained to her that she

needed to be as detailed as possible. She reassured her that nothing was too graphic. She told her she had heard a lot of detail in her years of listening to people's stories, and that adults are capable of acting totally disgusting and inappropriate things towards kids. If it happened to her, it happened to her. She was not at fault for any of it. She was a child. Even though she was 17, she was still a child. Jessica felt better knowing the lady felt that way. If she told her everything, there would be some disgusting parts. She dreaded it but knew it was necessary. She couldn't quit the process now, or she would surely be taken right back to her father. Aaron's words crept back in her mind, "He's not going to stop. You have to stop him." She finally agreed. She had to tell the lady everything.

Jessica talked to the psychologist for over an hour. She had been informed that the talk would be videotaped, but she never saw the video camera. She decided to tell every possible detail she could remember. It made her mad that there were times when the memories just stopped. She would have liked to have given *every* detail, but it was as though her mind turned off for a while then turned back on in spurts. When the interview was over, the psychologist left the room for a minute to talk to the others. She told Jessica to help herself to anything in the refrigerator. Of course, the refrigerator was packed with all kinds of food. Jessica wasn't hungry yet. She just wanted to take a peek.

The psychologist returned to the room, this time followed by the undercover police officer. The psychologist explained that Jessica was a very high priority case. She would need to be placed away from the home for a while. The police officer told her he had to call her mother to let her know that Jessica was safe but would not be returning home.

"You're not going to tell my mom what I told you, are you?" Jessica panicked.

The officer calmly spoke, "We are only going to tell her that you are in our custody, and she is not to worry about you. There will come a time when she will know more details, but my phone call will not be the time. If it would make you feel better, you can listen in on the call."

Jessica swallowed, "She's out of town with her sister and won't be back until Tuesday. I really don't want her to worry."

The officer informed her that he had to make the call but that he would be very brief and to the point. It was the law. Jessica wondered how he was able to get her aunt's phone number since she was in another state but didn't bother asking. The police officer made the call as Jessica listened in. She could tell her mother must have asked some questions but the officer would say, "I'm sorry, but I am not at liberty to discuss that with you right now, ma'am."

Jessica still felt a little anxious, but she also felt the biggest relief. She felt as though her secret was no longer the five hundred pound burden it had become. She still had a fear of the unknown, but that anxiety was blended with the relief of knowing all these grownups were on her side.

It was time to take her to the youth shelter where she would spend the night.

"But I don't have any clothes," Jessica admitted.

"Not to worry. We will get you some clothes," Matuschka reassured her.

Jessica told everyone, "Thank you so very much."

The youth shelter was another trip into the country. It was on the outskirts of town. It was more casual, and a lady greeted them at the door with a smile.

"Hi, my name is Kellie. I work the night desk. Please come in," she invited.

She looked barely older than Jessica, but she seemed really nice. They found Jessica a room to herself and some pajamas. She was told breakfast would be at 6:30. Kellie gave her a box of crackers and some raisins for a middle of the night snack. Someone would be by in the morning to wake her. Once she felt Jessica was comfortable with the arrangement, Matuschka said her "good byes." She hugged Jessica and told her that Kellie would take care of her the rest of the night. If she needed anything, Kellie would be there.

Jessica was glad she had her own room, but for the first time since she had called Mrs. Willingham, she felt alone. In a way it was a relief. She knew no one was going to hit her. No one was going to touch her inappropriately, and no one was going to make her touch someone else inappropriately. She was emotionally drained. Even though she didn't want to go to sleep, she did very quickly after she curled up in her bed.

Jessica stood near the swings at Hidden Park and looked up at the birds. The birds were happy and singing their playful songs. Jessica decided to join them. With the will of

her own thoughts she started flying with them -- smiling and laughing. She came near a cloud. As she looked at the cloud, a face formed – a face she recognized instantly – Aaron.

He spoke to her, "Jesse, my sweet-sweet Jesse. You did it! I am so happy for you. It will be a long process, but you can handle it. Always trust what's in your soul. You have all the answers you need right inside you."

As quickly as he appeared, he disappeared. Jessica called out to the sky, "When will I see you again?"

She didn't see him but heard his voice, "In time -- when everything is in alignment".

Jessica woke up very thirsty. She crawled out of bed and found the nearest bathroom. The best thing about the youth shelter was that there was always a light on and always someone at the front desk near the door. It made Jessica feel safe.

She crawled back into bed. Jessica drifted off to sleep thinking about her life and how she felt safe at the shelter. The feeling of safety was shattered by her next dream.

The police officer drove Jessica back to her home. Her mother was still gone, and her father met them at the front door. The police officer shook his head as though Jessica had lied to him and drove off. No one was around except Jessica and her father. Mr. Taylor looked at her and motioned her inside. She obediently followed. As soon as they were in the house the door slammed shut behind them. Mr. Taylor was standing in front of her looking at her, studying her intently. She felt uncomfortable but was paralyzed. She couldn't move. She couldn't talk. He reached out to put one of his hands over her mouth. She couldn't breathe very well. He undressed her with his other hand. She was ashamed but couldn't do anything to fight back. He pushed her onto the bed which appeared out of nowhere. He kept telling her it was her duty to please him and that she liked everything he did. He told her she had brought this on herself. This was her punishment for running away. He was now holding her arms down. They were over her head crossed at the wrist. He held them together with his iron grip. She couldn't move. Even though his hand was gone from her mouth, some invisible force kept her from being able to yell. She struggled under his weight and tried to scream but nothing came out. She was trapped -- nowhere to go -- no one to help her as he did the unthinkable. He penetrated her, and as he did she began to sob. He ignored her crying while he reached his own gratification. She had lost every ounce of value as he released her. He walked away leaving her lying on the bed naked, used, and ashamed. The only thing she could do was cry. Finally she regained some strength; she sat up and screamed, "You bastard, I hate you!"

Jessica awoke to find that she truly had sat up in bed and screamed. Her cheeks were wet from her tears. She was trembling. Kellie heard her scream and came running into her room to find Jessica crying in her bed.

"Nightmare?" she asked sympathetically.

Jessica nodded her head. Kellie whispered, "A lot of kids have them once they get here. You will be okay. You're safe here, sweetie." Kellie sat down and put her arm around her. Jessica melted into her arms and cried until she was down to her last tear. Though it was just a dream, she still felt disgusted and ashamed.

Chapter 12

Safe and Strong House

The next several days were a whirlwind for Jessica. She learned that while they were escorting her to the youth shelter, and she was getting settled in, authorities were actually in the process of obtaining an arrest warrant for Mr. Taylor.

The psychologist decided it was too traumatic for Jessica to go back to the same school, so they placed her in a program called Safe and Strong, a combination of identity protection and rehabilitation program. They thoroughly explained to Jessica how it was set up and managed. She was told it was a privately owned business that worked along with Child Protective Services. The main difference was that Safe and Strong was a place that had plenty of staff and was well funded. Its founder was a woman who endured a childhood filled with sexual, physical, and emotional abuse. She never told anyone while she was a child. When she became an adult, the scars from her past haunted her. She suffered for over a decade with horrific nightmares of the abuse that she tried to keep inside and forget about. The nightmares affected her relationships and her ability to enjoy life. She wanted better for herself so she decided to enter a counseling program. There she was able to tell her story without worrying about her abusers finding out. It took years, but she finally came to terms with it. In the process she realized how important it was to tell someone about her abuse. That's when she made it her mission to get victims to speak out.

She was already a successful business woman so she understood the importance of planning. She met with experts in many fields to get advice on how to best serve children coming out of abusive environments. She created an executive council made up of these experts to help oversee the structure and operation of a place designed especially for rehabilitating children coming out of abusive environments. Through this process the Safe and Strong Organization was born.

When a child enters the program, several things happen. First she is assigned to a surrogate mother and father and allowed to choose a new name. The surrogate family is a married couple who is hired by Safe and Strong to be "normal" parents to the child. They have been extensively trained and have a contract with Safe and Strong. The first year assigned to the child, the new-ly formed family must live at the facility in an on-campus apartment. One parent must be available for the child 24 hours a day. This is their job. They are there to give emotional support as well as to ensure that the child attends classes and the required counseling sessions.

The classes are set up to teach healthy habits for life. The classes are taught based on the child's age and development. Some of them include: Personal Health and Fitness, Nutrition and Cooking, and Appropriate Social Behaviors. In addition to these, the child is provided an hour of counseling each day with the on-site child psychologist and an hour of academic tutoring to match his or her grade in school.

Even though the day is extremely structured, a certain amount of free time is allowed. The Safe and Strong House has a playground, a bowling alley, a movie theatre, an indoor gym, and an indoor pool, as well as a large library on its grounds. The whole focus is to build back the child's self-esteem and give them a childhood. Phase I of the program takes a minimum of 30 days up to one full year to complete, depending on the needs of the individual victim. Phase I is when they get their lives back on track with the support of the Safe and Strong Staff. The non-abusing parent is allowed visitation rights, but only after completing a class on "Road to Recovery." In this class, the parent learns how to stand up for herself and her child against an abuser. Sadly enough, many of the non-abusing parents grew up in abusive environments themselves and are not aware of how to stop the cycle. This is their chance.

When the child reaches a certain level of functioning (determined by psychological testing), he or she may be moved to an independent satellite home to start Phase II. The Safe and Strong children are placed in these satellite homes with their surrogate parents. These homes are individual houses owned by Safe and Strong where each child is introduced back into mainstream society. The children start attending the school district in which the home is located and start getting involved in the local activities. At this transition, each child has the option of using the name she chose upon entering Safe and Strong or returning to her original name.

Once the child has adjusted to the new home with her surrogate parents, the non-abusing parent may increase the amount of time spent with his or her child (as long as all expectations of Safe and Strong have been met). The parent is coached by the child psychologist and by the surrogate parents to develop healthy parenting skills. The surrogate parents and the non-abusing parents work out a schedule that increases the amount of time the non-abusing parent lives at the house as the amount of time the surrogate parents live there is decreased. Eventually, the non-abusing parent lives full time at the house, and the surrogate parents are only "on call." Phase II lasts for six months to one school year.

Phase III is graduation and beyond. Upon graduation, the children are free to leave the satellite houses with their non-abusing parents. Of course, once a part of Safe and Strong, a child can always return to whatever phase he or she needs in order to continue healing. These children are part of the Safe and Strong family for life.

Phase IV is Forgiveness. This is the only time the abusing parent is allowed in the program. It is created based on the individual needs of the child and the mental health of the abusing adult. It is only put into effect at the unanimous request of the surrogate parents, the non-abusing parents, and the children.

Chapter 13

Moving On

Jessica truly enjoyed her time at Safe and Strong. When she entered Phase I and was allowed to pick out her new name, she chose Annie J. Howser. She was assigned to Sherry and John Foresman who became her surrogate parents. She was a little hesitant to open up to them even though she understood they were her surrogate parents. In time, however, she grew to love them. Being around John was very good for her because she saw first-hand a grown male who was warm and caring toward his wife. Even when he was angry, he never was disrespectful to Jessica or Sherry. It was the first time she had ever seen a full grown man control his temper when something didn't go his way. Sherry was a kind loving person as well. She was such a good listener and did everything she could to make Jessica feel like her own child. During Phase I of the program, they made sure Jessica took the appropriate classes, they scheduled time for her to spend with a personal trainer, and they made sure they took her out for ice cream after a her long intense sessions with her psychologist.

The roughest times were when Jessica would lie in her bed at night worrying about when she would see her mother again. She wished so much her mother could have found a man like John to marry. She wished her mother could experience that same kind of happiness that Sherry and John shared.   She appreciated the time and attention they gave her while she was spending time healing.

One thing she wasn't prepared for was her repeated nightmares. Since the day her father had tried to make Jessica touch him inappropriately, she had been having sickening nightmares. Every one of them had the same theme. Every one of them ended with her father raping her and telling her it was her duty as a daughter and that it was her fault. After every nightmare, she awoke screaming at him and bawling her eyes out. Fortunately, Sherry would always come in hold her until she calmed down. The only thing she ever said was, "It's over. You are safe now, Annie. He can't touch you anymore."

By the time Jessica completed Phase I, she had a daily routine of waking up at 6:00 a.m. and journaling for 30 minutes. She would change into exercise clothes and run with her trainer 5 miles. After showering she would eat breakfast with Sherry and John. She would spend an hour or two with her academic tutor to complete her high school courses. She would attend either her "Nutrition and Cooking" class or her "Human Behavior" class, depending on what day it was. At noon she would take her lunch out to the commons area and eat with another girl close to her age named Caroline. Then she would visit her psychologist in the afternoon. Afterwards she would go to an Art Class. She would then have supper with Sherry and John. The evenings allowed her some free time. Many nights Sherry and John would have some sort of family time scheduled. Sometimes they played board games; sometimes the went bowlin; other times they just watched television.

Life was good. Her mother even went

through the recommended classes so she was able to visit with Jessica a few times a week.

The day came for the transition into Phase II. She, Sherry, and John moved to a cute little house in a small town about two hours away from her home town. She enrolled and finished her senior year at the local high school. She transferred too late in the school year to try out for the cheerleading squad, but that was okay with her. During that time she started taking her ACT and SAT college entrance exams and also started applying for different colleges. Her mother's visits became more frequent during that time, and they talked for hours attempting to process what they had both learned in their time with Safe and Strong. Both of them agreed that everyone at Safe and Strong did all they could to help Jessica succeed.

When applying for college, she felt strong enough to go back to her real name. Even though it had been a little therapeutic to go by Annie, claiming her name back seemed like it sent the statement, "I, Jessica, have won!" Safe and Strong supported her decision.

In August she graduated from Safe and Strong, moved out of the satellite house she shared with her surrogate parents, and moved into a college dormitory. She felt free. It was the beginning of her adult life and what she had always longed for. She had a support team that included her mother, Sherry, John, and all the staff at Safe and Strong. She knew she was on her way to becoming a happy, healthy, successful woman. She never realized the stress her father's abuse had placed on her and her mother, but, now that she had been away from him for almost two years, she felt a peace she had never known before.

Jessica attended a four year university just a couple of hours away from her home town. She was actually reunited with several of her high school friends who went there too. Jessica was surprised one day several months into her freshman year to see Suzie strolling across campus. She had to do a double take to be certain, but, sure enough, it was her good friend from so long ago. Jessica ran after Suzie and tapped her on the back of her shoulder. Suzie turned and her face broke into a wide toothy grin. The girls immediately dropped their books and embraced.

"I thought you were gone for good! No one knew where you went. We just heard that you moved away," Suzie excitedly blurted out.

She stopped before saying anything about Jessica's father. Stillwater was a small enough town that things got around pretty quickly. Suzie knew Jessica's father was in jail. Neither girl talked about him.

"I'm so glad to know you are okay, Jessica. I worried about you so much." She continued.

"I'm in a healthier place now, trust me. I'm happy -- really happy," Jessica replied.

"Mark and I are engaged!" Suzie gushed, unable to contain her excitement any longer.

"Congratulations! When's the wedding?" Jessica inquired, excited for her friend.

"We decided to have a long engagement. We will get married the summer after we graduate from college. You had better be there!" Suzie replied.

"Wow! That is a long engagement. But if you know you are meant to be together, four years out of a lifetime isn't very long. I am so happy for you! Well, I need to get to class. Here is my number. I wouldn't miss the wedding for the world." Jessica scratched down her number on a piece of notebook paper torn from her spiral. "Give me a call. I missed you! You were a great friend to me."

The two girls embraced again and then went their separate ways. Seeing Suzie again made Jessica remember the night of the double date. She had met Mark's cousin, Steven. He was such a good guy, but they never saw each other again. She wondered what he was doing now over a year later.

Jessica walked on to class. She briefly thought about the attack after that date, but quickly reminded herself that it was over. Her father couldn't touch her now. Then she thought about Aaron. She had not had any real dreams of him since that night. Occasionally, his face would appear in a dream, but it was just a fleeting image. The dreams now weren't anything like what she had before -- when Aaron was alive. She looked up at the sky and softly spoke the words, "I love you, Aaron, wherever you are. I miss you the most."

As though her mind were speaking to her, she heard the words, "I know. I love you, too." Then the song, "Faithfully" by Journey flooded her senses once again. Even though they were only in her thoughts, she felt Aaron had sent the words and the song for her.

He had fulfilled his promise after all. He gave her the strength and encouragement to seek help. She would always be grateful for that. Now it was her turn to help others. She felt a burning desire to reach out to all who were hurting, just like she had hurt. She knew there were other children out there who were afraid to say anything about their secret hell. Now, she was the one on "the other side" in a position to hold out her hand. Her goal was, first, to get a degree in psychology, then to go out into the world and make a positive difference -- just like all those people who had made a positive difference in her life. It was her destiny to make life better for those younger than she who were travelling the same road.

Chapter 14

A Final Visit

It was the year 2008, twenty four years after Jessica had first reported her abuse to a trusted teacher, and it was the beginning of autumn. The wind was starting to blow harder and the leaves surrendered themselves to the currents that pushed them in different directions. A large Maple leaf spiraled down to the ground in Sunrise Memorial Gardens, the same cemetery Jessica had visited after Aaron's death. Mrs. Willingham parked her car near the office and stepped out, readjusting her sunglasses. The redness in her eyes revealed to anyone present that she had been crying. In her hands she daintily held two red roses. She set off on her mission. At the end of the school year, she would retire and move to Texas with her husband. She wanted to make one final visit to pay respect to her students. She found her way to the first headstone which read:

Aaron James Howser

1966-1983

A gust of wind lifted her hat from her head. She quickly retrieved it and secured it with her free hand. She closed her eyes for a moment as if in prayer then set a single rose across his grave. She blew him a motherly kiss and turned to search for another site. Finally she spotted what she was looking for and approached the final grave. She stopped to read the headstone which was much fancier than the first:

In Loving Memory

Jessica Ann Taylor 1967-2007

World Famous Author and Philanthropist

A woman who lived by Gandhi's words:

*"Be the **change** you want to see in the world."*

Mrs. Willingham wiped away a tear as she placed the second red rose across Jessica's grave. She blew another kiss into the wind and uttered, "Good bye, sweet children. May you both finally rest in peace."

Chapter 15

Alignment

Mrs. Taylor was sitting in the kitchen of her one bedroom cabin in Colorado. She was drinking her morning coffee before she headed off to work at the Safe and Strong office in Denver. After Jessica had moved away to college, Mrs. Taylor divorced Mr. Taylor and went back to work as secretary for a local business. Then one summer a job became available with the Safe and Strong organization. She applied and was thrilled when she was offered the position as office manager. After she worked there several years, the organization expanded so she and relocated to Colorado.

She was thumbing through the headlines of the Denver Post. She always read the first page then found the Obituaries and the Birth Announcements looking for people she knew. At the top if the paper, the date read April, 6, 2008.

Her cat started purring to be fed so she laid the paper on the table face up. She took the bag of cat food from the pantry and poured some into her cat's bowl. She chuckled as her cat became more excited at the sound of the pellets hitting the metal sides. She set the bowl on the ground and stroked the cat's back as it began to eat. She then took her seat back at the kitchen table. A name jumped off the page at her in the Birth Announcements.

She read:

Jessica Ann, *baby girl. Born to Matthew and JoDawn Thomas of Aurora, Colorado. Born at 1:23 a.m. weighing 6 lbs 3 oz.*

Mrs. Taylor sat for a moment, thinking about how wonderful her own Jessica Ann had been. She couldn't have asked for a better daughter who had a heart of gold. Even though it had been almost a year since her Jessica had lost her battle with breast cancer, Jessica was still greatly missed. With her right hand, Mrs. Taylor took hold of the cross necklace she wore around her neck. It was the last thing Jessica gave to her, and she held it close to her heart.

In Jessica's short 40 years, she had made an impact worldwide with her novels about breaking the silence in abusive homes and about breaking the cycles of abuse that run in families from generation to generation. Jessica had kept all her journals from her meetings with her psychologists and published her journey for millions to read. She also enjoyed public speaking and took great pleasure in speaking to large groups of people about respecting each other and about personal boundaries. She gave motivational speeches at a variety of conventions about living life to the fullest and loving who you are. She even made an appearance on the Oprah Show to spread her message.

Jessica had often revisited Safe and Strong to talk with the "newbies" about what life could be if they finished the program. She made it a priority to speak to legislators about unifying the laws nationwide on dealing with child abuse so children would experience the same process from Alaska to Hawaii and from Maine to California. She firmly believed that it would be easier for abused children too speak up and report their abuse if they knew what to expect. After she completed her stay at Safe and Strong she was horrified to find out other children may not have the same type of support in their communities. To help with this she bought buildings and donated them to communities so they could facilitate their own branch of the Safe and Strong organization. She bought homes to serve as satellite homes for rehabilitation. She made donations to multiple charities that provide services for people involved in domestic abuse. Her list of philanthropic deeds was endless.

Everyone who knew Jessica was devastated by the unexpected loss. She had touched so many lives in such a short period of time. Mrs. Taylor still missed her only baby. Months after her death, the Safe and Strong organization dedicated a library in their commons area in her memory. They called it the "Jessica Anne Taylor Library for Healing Hearts."

Mrs. Taylor took great comfort in thinking about all the wonderful and positive things Jessica had done in her life. Her thoughts were brought back into the present when her cat rubbed against her leg. She needed to get to work.

Mrs. Taylor laid the newspaper down on the table before reading a very important part. There was a small section that could possibly have eased her pain of losing Jessica too soon. It was a birth announcement that was listed several announcements down.

It read:

Aaron James, *baby boy, Born to Patrick and Kimberly Hatfield of Englewood, Colorado. Born at 2:34 a.m. weighing 7 lbs 11 oz.*

Aaron was the one aspect of Jessica's life Mrs. Taylor never really knew about. She never knew a single lifetime was merely a blink of an eye for Jessica and Aaron. She never knew that their two souls were destined to love for an eternity. She never knew that Jessica and Aaron were, and forever will be, soul mates.

The End....?

Dear Readers,

I thank you from the bottom of my heart for reading my book.

To be honest, publishing this story is one of the hardest things I've ever done. It is like slicing open my midsection and allowing everyone to see what's inside. Though the book is a work of fiction, I have included a lot of my own thoughts, feelings, and experiences. I used each of the characters to be my voice to represent different parts of my own   journey.

Since I published this myself, I'm sure there are mistakes that I failed to catch. Regardless of those mistakes, it is more important to me that my message is heard loud and clear. If you are someone in an abusive situation, you must find a person of authority who can help you. None of us makes it alone in this life; we all must work together to help our fellow brothers and sisters. Reporting abuse is not a sign of weakness; rather, it is a sign of strength.

There are many organizations set up to help. Keeping abuse a secret not only hurts you, but could negatively affect how you treat your own children someday. For their sake, get the help you need. I spent seven years in counseling to deal with the shame of abuse in my childhood. Those seven years gave me tools to deal with my own emotions. The counseling allowed me to be the best mother I could be to my children and the best wife I could be to my husband. Seven years is a long time, but to become a healthy, happy person for my family, it was well worth it. My husband and daughters mean the world to me.

No matter who you are or what your story is, I hope you fight for your "happily ever after" regardless of how long it takes to find it.

Sincerely,
D.S. Baze